## "Mind if I join you?" Matt asked seductively

His voice was teasing, but Casey wasn't playing this game with him anymore. Not after this morning. She was attracted to him. Wanted him.

She smiled back, brushing a lock of hair from her damp cheek. "Suit yourself." Casey waved her hand over the bathtub.

He looked at her in surprise and she was delighted that she had finally rendered Matt Garrison speechless. She watched as his eyes moved down to the beads of water glittering on her shoulders and chest.

"Well?" she asked. "Are you going to join me?"

Matt's attention snapped back to her face. "No...thanks. I just stopped by to see how you were doing, and pick up my camera." He paused. "I left it in the bedroom," he added lamely.

Casey closed her eyes and slid more deeply into the tub, listening to his movements in the bedroom. She knew now, without a doubt, she had the power to beat Matt Garrison at his own game!

**Kate Hoffmann** is a real find. Every year, Temptation holds a contest for the unpublished members of Romantic Writers of America, and Kate was the winner of the 1992 contest! Kate began writing about four years ago when she decided the only way to find the perfect romance novel was to write it herself. She began writing a historical novel, but as soon as she picked up a Harlequin Temptation she was hooked. After reading about forty Temptation novels in three months Kate began *Indecent Exposure*. The idea for the book came out of Elizabeth Taylor's latest marriage and all the media hoopla surrounding it. Like every good writer she wondered "what if..." We're proud to welcome Kate Hoffmann to the wonderful lineup of authors at Harlequin Temptation. Truly she is "a voice of tomorrow."

# INDECENT EXPOSURE

**KATE HOFFMANN**

*Harlequin Books*

TORONTO • NEW YORK • LONDON
AMSTERDAM • PARIS • SYDNEY • HAMBURG
STOCKHOLM • ATHENS • TOKYO • MILAN
MADRID • WARSAW • BUDAPEST • AUCKLAND

To the Tuesday night ladies—
Sue, Lori, Susie, Leslie, Rasma, Ann and Georgann

Published August 1993

ISBN 0-373-25556-X

INDECENT EXPOSURE

Printed in U.S.A.

# 1

*The voice on the phone said, "Noon, the Palisades Hotel on Tremont, room 429." I arrived to find the lobby empty. The hotel was as flea-bitten as a junkyard dog. Room 429 wasn't hard to find; it was the one with the shiny new dead-bolt lock. The lock took twenty-four seconds. As I pushed open the door the smell of murder hit me like a northbound train on a southbound track. There was no blood and no body, but I laid ten to one that Willy the Weasel would turn up on some beach tomorrow and he wasn't going to be there for his tan. Someone had gotten to him before I could, and that someone probably knew more about me now than my mother. That's the problem with L.A. There are no secrets; everyone has his price.*

*By the way, my name is Theodora Thibidoux and I'm a private investigator.*

THE HOTEL CORRIDOR was silent. Casey Carmichael slipped out of the broom closet at the end of the long, elegantly appointed hallway and walked toward room 631. She ticked off the room numbers in her mind and as she passed each door, the tempo of her pulse increased. When she got within sight of her destination, her heart felt ready to burst and her knees wobbled.

"Theodora," she whispered, her gaze darting between the door of the room and the elevator at the end of the hall. "Where are you when I really need you?"

Casey drew a deep but shaky breath and pushed her horn-rimmed glasses up the bridge of her nose. She stopped before the gilt-and-white door labeled 631, withdrew the room key from the pocket of the ill-fitting maid's uniform and with trembling hands reached for the doorknob.

"Just stay calm," she murmured to herself. "Stay calm."

Suddenly her actions felt suspended in time, excruciatingly slow and deliberate. The grate of the key against the door seemed to echo through the hall, loudly enough to reach the guests in the penthouse suite, five stories above.

Hurry, she chanted inwardly, but her nerve-numbed fingers refused to work properly. Just as the key moved into the lock, it slipped from her grasp, tumbled end over end, and landed on the plush carpet at her feet. With a tiny moan of frustration, she bent to retrieve her ill-gotten treasure.

Fireworks exploded before her eyes as her nose and the doorknob met head-on. The shock of the impact caused her to cry out, and with a silent curse, she hopped from foot to foot, waiting for the pain to subside and her watery eyes to clear. Why was she always clumsy when she was nervous? Why couldn't she be cool under pressure?

Casey felt a hysterical giggle working its way through her throat. "Reporter Loses Nose to Hotel Doorknob." "Knob Wins, Nose Goes." "Noseless Writer Sniffs Out Another Scandal."

Since she had started writing for *The Inquisitor*, passing thoughts frequently took the form of sensational headlines. Everyday situations seemed ripe with outlandish story possibilities. Her normally well-controlled and focused imaginative powers had gone completely haywire. Alien babies, giant sharks, and Bigfoot had usurped Theodora Thibidoux, the heroine of her still-unpublished detective novels.

It was only right, Casey thought. After all, Theodora had yet to bring in a dime. Bigfoot, on the other hand, had paid the rent last month.

The thought of her dwindling finances brought her mind back to the task at hand. Rubbing her nose and straightening her crooked glasses, she snatched the key from the floor and forced it into the lock. Though the Do Not Disturb sign hung from the knob, she knew the room was unoccupied. The greedy little bellman, Eddie, had thrown in that valuable bit of information as a bonus—after she had paid him one hundred dollars for the room key.

After two years in the tabloid business, she was still amazed at how easily confidential information could be purchased. Everyone had a price and anyone could be bought.

Including me, she thought with a twinge of guilt. For twenty-five thousand dollars a person could forget her own high standards of right and wrong. A person could turn into a cynic or a mercenary. A person could even find herself breaking into a hotel room to snoop through a man's personal belongings.

The lying and deception that usually went along with dishing celebrity dirt always made her uncomfortable. Unlike her peers at *The Inquisitor*, she felt dishonest creating a scandalous story about real people just to sell papers. So she had created a niche at *The Inquisitor* with her "human interest" stories—bizarre retellings of alien encounters, miracle cures for baldness and heroic actions by the family dog. Though her stories didn't make very hot copy, at least they didn't hurt anyone; they were harmless entertainment and easy to research. Unlike the other reporters, Casey avoided pounding the pavement in search of a celebrity indiscretion and did most of her investigating by phone.

Until today.

Melvin Finkleman, Hollywood's most powerful business manager, had left his room at the Beverly Palms Hotel nearly thirty minutes ago. Destination? The office of Dr. Lance Reed, Hollywood's most popular plastic surgeon. By the end of the day, half the tabloids in the country would know whether Melvin, or one of his famous clients, would be going under the knife. But she wasn't interested in that story. She had bigger stars to catch, namely Melvin's most famous client, Emily Harrington.

Casey pushed the door open and stepped inside the darkened room. The heavy drapes drawn together reduced the brilliant noonday California sun to a mere sliver of light. The faint sound of the traffic on Wilshire Boulevard drifted up from the street. She flipped on the light and quickly scanned the room.

Papers were strewn across the unmade bed and nearly buried the reproduction Louis Quatorze desk. Clothes lay in heaps on the floor. Two room-service trays on the coffee table held the remnants of a lavish breakfast. A red brassiere hung from the lamp.

"Melvin Finkleman," Casey said softly, a tiny smile tugging at her lips, "you naughty, naughty boy. No wonder Mrs. Finkleman kicked you out." Mrs. Finkleman's intolerance for infidelity and her husband's penchant for blowsy starlets had been an incredible stroke of luck. The Finkleman estate was a fortress, inaccessible to even the finest tabloid reporters. But the Beverly Palms, known affectionately at *The Inquisitor* as the "Greased" Palms, had four employees on the paper's snitch list. One phone call to Eddie and she was on her way to realizing her dream.

It was as if fate had played a hand in bringing her here. During last week's editorial meeting, Art Griswold, the tabloid's owner, had dangled the bait. Emily Harrington, the hottest young actress to hit Hollywood since Monroe, was getting married. His source was solid, and he had paid big bucks to keep the tip under wraps. The two-year-old *Inquisitor*, an upstart in the competitive tabloid market, would break the exclusive story and finally take its proper place on the supermarket racks. To insure his success, Art had offered a twenty-five-thousand-dollar bonus to the reporter who brought in the story and photos. Casey planned to be that reporter.

Carefully, Casey rummaged through the papers on the desk, looking for any bit of information that would help her track down the elusive Emily. A quick examination of the contents of Melvin's open briefcase yielded nothing of importance. As she opened the drawers of the desk, an airline ticket propped up against the reading lamp drew her attention. She pulled the voucher out of the folder and studied it closely: LAX to Denver, WestAir Flight 205, departing this Friday, 2:45 p.m., passenger V. Leslie.

Pulling a piece of hotel stationery out of the top drawer, she scribbled the information across the paper. There was a connecting flight, from Denver to Laramie. The name on the ticket was oddly familiar, and as she studied the voucher more carefully, realization dawned. Victoria Leslie, the heroine of the award-winning movie, *The Gods of Love,* aka Emily Harrington, the hottest actress in Hollywood and one half of the "Wedding of the Year." She had what she came for.

"Oh, Melvin. You are a clever man, but not clever enough." Casey kissed the ticket before putting it carefully back in its place. As she started toward the door, she caught a glimpse of herself in the mirror on the closet door. The starched maid's cap she had hastily pinned to her hair was slightly askew, and several errant auburn curls hung down over her left shoulder. As she paused to pin the cap in place, she heard the sound of a key in the lock.

Her heart lurched. Frantically she searched for a place to hide. The bed was halfway across the room and she doubted whether she could get underneath it without being caught. For a brief moment, she thought about hiding in the shower. In the end, she stepped into the huge walk-in closet, just as the door to the room swung open.

The closet was dark and smelled of stale cigar smoke. Casey crinkled her nose, fighting the urge to sneeze. On the other side of the door she could hear the sound of rustling papers. The odor of a lighted cigar drifted under the closet door. Melvin was back!

Why hadn't she just stayed in the room and pretended to be the maid? And why did she think of that now when she was *inside* the closet? If he found her hiding in the closet, he would call the police. She'd be charged with breaking and entering and be locked up in the Beverly Hills jail. Her name would be in all the papers and her career would be ruined.

Her career? What career? Working for *The Inquisitor* wasn't really a career. It was simply a means to an end, a way to pay the rent and continue working on her "Theodora" detective novels. Getting this story would put an end to her illustrious job as a tabloid journalist. It would give her the money to buy her dream—a real home and a real career.

Casey opened the closet door slightly and peeked through the thin crack. Melvin was moving in her direction. She stepped back into the folds of his clothing until her back rested against the rear wall of the closet. He was going to find her. She was certain of it now.

But he didn't open the closet door. Instead, she saw his figure pass the narrow stream of light shining through the crack. The room door opened and then closed. She waited several moments more before she stepped forward to peek out again. When she could hear no other noise, she poked her head out of the closet and breathed a heavy sigh of relief.

The room was empty. Melvin was gone.

"Thank God," she said out loud.

"Is he gone?" asked a deep masculine voice behind her. With a scream, she scrambled out of the closet, slammed the door and braced her shoulder against it.

Her heart was pounding and her breath came in shallow gasps. Who the devil was in the closet? She put her ear up against the door and waited for her captive to say something, but when he didn't she wondered whether her mind was playing tricks on her. Maybe she had imagined the voice. There wasn't anyone in the closet, she reasoned. It's just nerves.

"Are you still out there?" the muffled voice called.

She wasn't dreaming. There *was* a man in the closet. And she had been in there with him for the past five minutes.

"What are you doing in there?" she asked, trying to sound authoritative but failing miserably.

"I could ask you the same thing."

"I'm asking the questions here," she shouted. "Now either answer my question or I'll call hotel security."

"You won't call security."

Casey thought she detected a note of smugness in his voice. "I'm calling security now," she shot back.

"No, you aren't." He pushed against the door as if to prove his statement.

Wedging her foot against the bottom of the door, she tried to reach the desk chair with an outstretched arm, determined to jam it under the doorknob and trap the man inside. But the chair stood just beyond her fingertips. She braced her back against the door and dug her heels into the carpet, but as the door was firmly pushed from the other side, she began to slide across the floor. When the door was open about a foot, a hand emerged and grabbed for her. In her effort to avoid his grasp, she lost her balance. Her captive gave one final shove, forced the door wide open and sent her sprawling across the floor.

From the floor, she watched him cross the room, his long legs clad in faded blue jeans. When he picked up the phone, Casey allowed her gaze to drift upward, from his well-worn cowboy boots, along his muscular calves and thighs, past his narrow hips and across his wide back and shoulders. She stopped at his dark hair, curled over the collar of his beat-up leather jacket.

"Hotel security, please."

Her first instinct was to run for the door until she realized that he probably wanted her out of the room. If he was after her story, she wasn't about to oblige him. She smiled to herself. Maybe she wasn't half-bad at this detective stuff. Wouldn't Theodora be proud?

Casey jumped to her feet, closed the distance between them in an instant and grabbed the phone away from his ear.

"Put that phone down! Do you want to get us both thrown in jail?" She slammed the phone into its cradle, barely missing the finger that held the button down.

Ha! He had been bluffing. Her waning confidence quickly returned and she knew she now had the upper hand. Slowly he turned around, and as quickly as it had appeared, she felt her newly-won advantage dissolve into thin air.

Casey drew a sharp breath as she looked up into his eyes. They were incredibly blue, like the Pacific on a perfect summer day, and she was momentarily transfixed, unable to draw away from his bold gaze. Her eyes skimmed over the planes and angles of his face, the tanned contours darkened by the stubble of his beard. Her gaze was drawn to a thin scar on his chin, the only flaw in his perfect face. It gave him a strangely dangerous look. She realized she was staring, and a warm flush crept up her cheeks.

A smile played at the corners of his sensuous mouth and a glitter of amusement sparkled in his sapphire eyes as his own gaze strayed up and down her body. He was obviously aware of the effect he had on women and he was using it to his advantage.

"Casey Carmichael," he said, his voice both smooth and rough, like raw silk. It was more a statement than a question.

Casey looked at him in surprise, shifting uncomfortably under his candid appraisal. "How did you know my name?"

He ignored her question, walked over to one of the chairs that flanked the windows and sat down. With his long legs crossed in front of him, he slouched down comfortably. He didn't seem to be much of a threat now. Though he stood nearly a head taller than she, he wasn't nearly as intimidating when seated.

"Let me give you a little piece of advice, Casey. I wouldn't trust Eddie the bellman with any national secrets if I were you. That guy would sell his own mother for a ten spot."

Casey bristled at his patronizing attitude, then realized what he was telling her. "Ten dollars? That little weasel! When I get hold of—"

"Hey, give the little weasel a break. You'd talk too if you were about to be tossed down an elevator shaft. Anyway, I get first crack at him. He told me I'd have at least fifteen minutes before you got here."

Casey looked him squarely in the eyes, gathering her courage and trying to quell the uneasy feelings this man stirred in her. "Who *are* you? What are you doing here? And how did you know I was here?"

"Who, what, how. Griswold told me you were a good reporter. I'm impressed. Name's Matt Garrison." He held out his hand and Casey attempted a withering look. He laughed. "I'm a free-lance photographer. Whenever I'm a little short on cash, Art gives me work."

Casey regarded him warily. "How come I've never seen you around the office?"

"I don't spend much time in L.A. and when I do, I like to keep a low profile. My reputation as a serious photojournalist would be compromised if it got out that I was doctoring pictures of dog-faced boys at *The Inquisitor*."

"How did you know I was here?"

He reached into his pocket and pulled out a crumpled piece of paper. "You really shouldn't leave your notes lying out in the open for everyone to see. You never know when one of your unscrupulous coworkers might rifle through your garbage."

Casey snatched the paper from his hand and looked down at it in disbelief. It was her notepaper, with Eddie's name scrawled across the paper, the hotel name and Melvin's room number right below it. "You went through my garbage?"

He shrugged. "Garbage is a tabloid reporter's best source of information." He pulled her desk key out of his pocket and handed it to her. "I found this in the top drawer of your desk. Smart place to hide your desk key. You might want to lock up your garbage from now on."

"You went through my garbage and you broke into my desk. How dare you! You've got the journalistic ethics of a . . . a worm."

"Hey, didn't anyone tell you we don't use the *E* word in the tabloid industry? Besides, when it comes to money, my ethical standards drop a few degrees. And who are you to call me names? Garbage is in the public domain. *You* bought a key, *you* broke into this room, and *you* went through a man's personal papers. I guess it takes a worm to know a worm."

Casey glared at him, sorely tempted to reach out and slap that smug look right off his handsome face. "What do you want? What are you doing here?"

"I'm here for the same reason you are—the twenty-five-thousand-dollar bonus. So why don't you make it easier for me and tell me what you found. Us worms hate legwork."

So he *was* after her story! Obviously Matt Garrison was just as determined to snag the bonus as she was, and he had no scruples when it came to ferreting out information. She would have to put a stop to his interference immediately. He was not going to take her twenty-five thousand.

"This is my story," Casey said in a firm, even voice. "I'm not going to let you—"

She stopped suddenly as she saw his gaze shift to the door. In the next instant, she heard the sound of a key in the lock. She stood frozen, unable to speak, unable to move. He was staring at her with those intense blue eyes and she hoped he had an excuse for their presence in the room, for she certainly didn't.

In one fluid motion, he grabbed her arm, pulled her down into his lap, and removed her glasses. She watched in alarm, her eyes wide, as his lips descended on hers and covered her open mouth with a scorching kiss. Casey frantically pushed against his chest, but he only tightened his embrace. As the door opened, he deepened the kiss, his tongue gently assaulting hers, his mouth moving erotically over her lips. Her mind began to whirl and she surrendered herself to the kiss, the sound of her pounding heart blotting out the sounds of angry voices at the door. Just when she thought she would pass out from lack of oxygen, Matt drew back and looked deeply into her eyes.

Trust me, his gaze said. I know what I'm doing.

Breathless, she gave him a tentative smile and a nod. She would have to trust him. She had no choice. But she certainly wasn't foolish enough to make a habit of it.

With a lazy grin, he looked up at the door. She watched as his expression turned from sleepy satisfaction to a look of surprise and shock. When she saw his face color in embarrassment, she marveled at his improvisational abilities, but her admiration was cut short when he stood up. She tried to grab his hand, but he pulled away and crossed his arms in a defensive posture over his chest, while she fell unceremoniously to the floor for the second time that day.

"What the hell are you doing in my room?" Melvin Finkleman stood in the doorway. Beside him, a skinny man in an impeccably tailored suit eyed them suspiciously. Casey guessed he was the hotel manager.

"Are these people friends of yours, Mr. Finkleman?" the manager said in a pretentious voice.

"I've never seen them before in my life."

Matt looked down at Casey, then held out his hand to pull her up beside him. He leaned closer to her, but kept his gaze on the irate pair at the door and spoke in a whisper designed to carry across the room. "Lurleen, honey," he drawled, "I thought you said we'd be alone."

Startled, Casey opened her mouth to blurt out an answer, but when she felt him squeeze her hand, she closed her mouth. She wasn't much for improvisation, anyway.

Matt dragged her toward the door and she followed obediently. "Mister, I'm sorry," he began, his drawl more pronounced. "It's all my fault. My little Lurleen was just tryin' to do her job. See, we had a little set-to this morning before she left for work and seein' as how I'm leavin' town for a few days, I had to put things right. I busted in here to find her and—well, you know how women can be. Sometimes they just can't get enough of a guy." Casey watched in fascination as the angry faces of Finkleman and the hotel manager softened slightly. They actually believed this line!

"Come on, honey," he said, giving her a solicitous little pat on the rear end and sliding her glasses back on her nose. "We'll just mosey on out of here and let these nice men take care of their business." He nudged Casey toward the door, and with a rush of relief she realized they were going to get out of the room unscathed.

"Wait just one minute." The hotel manager grabbed her arm viciously as she passed and yanked her around to face him. Matt came to an abrupt halt, his icy gaze locked on the manager's hand. A prickle of fear ran down her spine as she saw the hard look in his eyes.

He took a single menacing step toward the manager. "Kindly take your hands off my wife, mister," he said, his voice cold and remote, his drawl gone.

The hotel manager snatched his hand away and rubbed his palms together as if he'd been burned. He looked down his beak-like nose at Casey. "Lurleen, is it? Lurleen, after you show your husband the door, you will report immediately to my office. This is not the kind of behavior we allow at the Beverly Palms."

"Yes, sir," Casey mumbled, sliding past him, her hand still wrapped tightly in Matt's. "Right away, sir. Come on, darlin'." Dragging Matt along after her, she hurried out the door and closed it behind them.

In the safety of the hallway, her knees and her nerves gave way. Matt pulled her to him and held her close. She placed her forehead on his chest and drew in a deep breath. Her fingers splayed across the front of his T-shirt and felt the rippled muscle beneath. "We did it," she said in a trembling voice.

"Lurleen, honey," Matt whispered, his voice low and seductive, his breath teasing at her ear, "I think you and I had better hightail it out of here before the manager and Melvin realize what we were really doing in that hotel room."

Suddenly aware that she was wrapped in his arms, Casey looked up at him in embarrassment and watched a bemused, boyish grin break across his face. What was she doing? This guy was after her story and here she was, falling into his arms.

She pulled away from him and stalked down the hall, leaving him leaning against the wall outside room 631. As she rushed down the six flights of stairs, she heard his footsteps behind her. She ran out the door that led to the alley, ripped off the maid's cap and tossed it into a Dumpster. The ruffled apron followed. It was too late to retrieve the clothes she'd left in the broom closet, and she needed to escape Matt Garrison's disturbing presence as quickly as possible.

He followed several steps behind as she made her way to the street. "You stay away from me," she shouted over her shoulder. "This is *my* story, so just let it go."

"Your story? Who died and made you William Randolph Hearst? I have as much right to this story as you."

Casey stopped dead in her tracks; her shoulders stiffened and she clenched her fists. It took every shred of her willpower to refrain from turning on the guy and punching him in that perfectly chiseled nose of his. "Just stay away from me," she warned.

"I intend to get this story, Carmichael."

"What makes you think you can scoop me on this one?" she asked, spinning around to meet his gaze.

"Who got into Melvin's room first? For just ten dollars, I might add. And who managed to keep us from spending the night in the slammer? I'd say I already have the advantage. Face it, you can't do this alone. You need me."

"What are you trying to say? Are you implying that I don't have the brains to get this story? Or is it my experience that's lacking?"

He opened his mouth and Casey prepared herself for an onslaught of disparaging remarks about her abilities as a journalist. But to her surprise, he shut his mouth and smiled at her instead. A tingle of attraction shot through her but she smothered it immediately.

"I'm saying we make a great team," he said, his voice softening. "Together we could get this story."

"I don't need you!" she said, stamping her foot.

"Let's put it this way, darlin'," he said, affecting his irritating Texas drawl. "What would you rather have? Half of twenty-five thousand dollars, or all of nothing?"

"I'll take my chances." With that, she turned and stalked down the sidewalk. "And don't call me darlin'!" she shouted, before disappearing from view.

FIVE MINUTES LATER, Matt Garrison still stood in the alleyway, Casey's retreat running through his mind. He could vividly recall the gentle sway of her slender hips as she stalked away. He could almost feel the silkiness of the copper-colored curls that had tumbled loose when she pulled off the cap.

For a moment he had been tempted to go after her, to pull her back into his arms and lose himself in the incredible feel of her. At first glance, she looked like the prim and proper old maid that office gossip claimed she was. But one kiss was all it took to dispel that inaccurate impression. Behind those horn-rimmed glasses were a pair of green eyes in which passion glittered like sunlight on the surface of a lake.

He remembered her response as he kissed her, the tiny sounds of protest that caught in her throat and then dissolved, the tentative touch of her tongue on his, and he felt a tightening in his groin. She was so soft, so warm. The scent of her was like nothing he'd ever smelled before, pure and sweet like springtime and flowers. In the space of less than an hour, the lovely Casey Carmichael had managed to get under his skin.

He shook his head. He had been too long without a woman. Six solitary months in Nepal and not a willing female within five hundred kilometers. He was like a sailor on shore leave, jumping at the first woman that walked into view.

Casey Carmichael was far from his type. He preferred the dazzling, voluptuous types to the slender, bookish types; the kind of women who were easy to seduce and even easier to leave. Though his well-honed seductive techniques had come in handy in the past, he doubted they would work on Casey. Besides, he didn't want her warm, willing body nearly as much as he wanted the information she possessed. Information that would guarantee him a twenty-five-thousand-dollar bonus. Information that would buy him his dream.

From his hiding place in the closet, he had known she had found something. But what? He had been in Finkleman's room for only a few seconds before he'd heard the sound of her fumbling at the door. His ploy to send her running hadn't worked. She was obviously made of stronger stuff than he'd thought. And their hasty exit had left him no time to search the room himself.

So she had won round one. Advantage Carmichael. She had a lead on the Harrington story and he had nothing. Except an advantage of his own. Casey Carmichael was a rookie when it came to the down-and-dirty part of tabloid reporting. And she had no idea what he was capable of when it came to getting a story.

*So why not take the easy road, Garrison? Let her do all the work. Just gain her trust and don't let her out of your sight. Then, as soon as the story is in your hand, check the little piece of baggage and take off—twenty-five thousand dollars richer.*

He grinned as he walked down the alleyway toward the street. The plan was certainly worth considering. After all, Matt Garrison was not one to back down from a challenge and getting Casey Carmichael to trust him could prove to be a very interesting and rewarding challenge indeed.

# 2

*I've never been much for a man with a pretty face. The way I see it, men weren't meant to be drop-dead gorgeous. But this guy was. He was the kind of gorgeous that could curl a girl's toes. "Theodora," he said to me in that voice like melted chocolate, "Long time, no see." He was looking at me like it had been too long, way too long. I knew I couldn't trust him. I should have walked out of that smoky bar that instant, but I didn't. There was something about those eyes of his. Blue, like the Pacific on a perfect summer da—*

"OH, LORD," Casey said in a strangled whisper.

"You have something to add, Carmichael?" Art Griswold's booming voice pulled her out of her daydream and back into the middle of another of his long-winded editorial pep talks. She glanced up from the notepad she was doodling on and found her co-workers staring at her in annoyance and Art watching her over the top of his bifocals.

"No—no," she replied. "I'm sorry, please, go on."

Griswold picked up where he had left off, rattling on in one of his First Amendment soliloquies, rhapsodizing about the power of the press and bringing truth to the masses. Jeff Dugan, the reporter who sat to her left, gave her a sharp kick beneath the conference table.

"Nice going, Carmichael," he muttered. "He was winding down until you chimed in. Now we're going to hear that whole Watergate thing all over again. I think Griswold is actually under the delusion that he's running a real newspaper here."

Casey shifted in her chair, ignoring his chiding, and let her eyes drift down to her notes. *Like the Pacific on a perfect summer day.* The words had appeared out of nowhere, as if some perverse writer's muse had taken control of her fingers and willed them to scribble the traitorous combination of letters. She hadn't been aware of the words forming under her fingers, but the evidence was right in front of her.

Since she had left Garrison in the alley behind the Beverly Palms three hours ago, she had waged a constant battle to keep her thoughts from wandering in his direction. Even Griswold's lecture and Theodora's exploits couldn't occupy her mind for more than a moment.

What was it about Matt Garrison? He was everything she carefully avoided in the male of the species—arrogant, opinionated, and oh-so-charming. A man like that was trouble, all tied up in an incredibly pretty package. And though her experience with men was sadly limited, she knew instinctively that he was not to be trusted. He was the enemy. And he was out to steal her one chance at happiness.

Casey picked up her notepad and fiercely crossed out the last sentence. *Green*, she wrote. *Like the...fifteenth fairway at Pebble Beach.* She crossed the clumsy simile out as well and turned her attention back to Griswold.

"Hot copy," he said, emphasizing the words with his hands. "That's what sells papers. Stories that sizzle, photos that speak to the reader. That's what we need here." He ran his stubby fingers through his wiry gray hair, making it stand on end, as if he had just been struck by lightning. His tie was loose and his wrinkled shirt was stretched tightly over his rotund midsection.

Rumor had it that Griswold had once been city editor at *The Boston Globe,* but had taken a fall for the paper in a messy libel suit. Now he ran the struggling tabloid out of a suite of stuffy offices in Culver City, serving as both publisher and editor. Casey had begun working for the gruff but lovable man two months after she had arrived in Los Angeles.

She had hoped for a job at *The Times* or even at one of the smaller suburban newspapers. But the job market was tight and Casey had just five years' experience at a small-town Wisconsin paper to her credit. She was as desperate for a writing job as Griswold was to find a competent reporter.

The day he hired her, Art had also appointed himself Casey's mentor and guardian, and watched over her as a father would his favorite child. And Casey slipped into the role of daughter, taking the irascible old bachelor under her wing and cooking dinner for him on occasion, glad of the company.

So she settled into professional life at *The Inquisitor.* And to make up for her lack of a social life, she concentrated on her longtime dream of becoming a novelist. Theodora Thibidoux had been born out of boredom and loneliness.

There had been a few men along the way: smooth, West Coast types, handsome and self-absorbed, interested in purely superficial relationships and not in the long term. But even after two years in California, she still felt displaced, a fish out of water, a stranger in paradise. She longed for the quiet of northern Wisconsin, the rustle of the wind in the trees, the sound of the lake lapping against the shore. She was tired of the smog and the traffic, the isolation in the midst of bumper-to-bumper people.

At least now there was hope. If all went well, she would snag the bonus and make her escape. She would return to the one place she could call home.

Griswold was wrapping up his speech, and Casey grabbed her notes, ready to leave the minute he gave the word. But she was stopped by the appearance of a tall figure in the doorway of the conference room. All eyes turned to observe Matt Garrison as he took the chair next to Griswold. His gaze fixed on Casey and he gave her a disarming smile and a provocative wink. All eyes shifted simultaneously to her and Casey felt her face color. She dipped her head, hoping to hide her reaction to his unspoken greeting. But her gaze was drawn back to his face as soon as he turned to Griswold. A vivid picture of their encounter in the hotel room swam into her mind. She remembered the feel of his mouth on hers and unconsciously she touched her tongue to her upper lip, wondering if the taste of him still remained there.

Art turned to Matt and slapped him on the back. "I want to introduce all of you to an old friend of mine. This is Matt Garrison, a helluva photojournalist. He got us those pictures on the killer croc in Australia last year and those photos of the two-hundred-year-old man in Tibet the year before. Matt's going to be working on the Harrington wedding along with the rest of you. So my advice is to keep one eye on Emily and the other eye on your back," Griswold joked.

"Good advice," Jeff Dugan muttered. "That's the guy who scooped me on my eight-legged-cow story. Last time he was in town, we went out for a few beers and I told him about the story. A week later, his photo shows up on the front page. He'd scoop his own mother if it made him a buck."

Casey looked over at Dugan and then across the conference table at Matt. He was watching her, a smug smile curling his lips. So she had been right. Matt Garrison was not to be trusted.

As the meeting broke up, Casey tried to lose herself in the small crowd heading for the door, hoping to avoid another confrontation with Garrison. She was almost out of the room when Griswold called her name, caught her hand and drew her over to Matt.

"Carmichael, come here. I want you to meet Garrison."

Casey ground her teeth and pasted a smile on her face. "We've already met."

"Good, good. Then you won't mind entertaining Matt tonight. I have a meeting with my tax accountant and Matt just got into town this morning. He's been sleeping in airports and eating junk food for three days.

He could use a nice home-cooked meal. Why don't you make him that chicken thing you made for me a few Sundays ago?"

Casey swallowed convulsively. "I—I can't. I have plans for tonight."

Griswold waved her excuse off. "Then cancel them. I want you two to get to know each other. If you're determined to go after the Harrington story, Garrison could give you a few pointers. Hell, you might even think about working together. With your words and his pictures, there's no telling how many papers we could sell."

"A partnership," Matt exclaimed. "I've been trying to sell Carmichael on that idea, Art. I think she could really benefit from my expertise."

"Excuse me," Casey said in a choked voice, trying to control her temper. "I'll be right back." She turned from the pair, hurried out the door and rushed to the safety of her tiny cubicle in the large, airless room that housed *The Inquisitor*'s staff of reporters. She sat down at her desk and buried her burning face in ice-cold hands.

The nerve of that guy! He was using his friendship with Art to worm his way into her good graces. How dare he try to manipulate her like that! Why couldn't he just leave her alone and turn his attention to one of the other women in the office? From the cow-eyed looks they had given him in the meeting, she was certain any one of the girls would be delighted to spend time with Matt Garrison.

Casey took a deep breath and pushed away from her desk. Her gaze dropped to the baggy jumper and T-shirt she wore and then drifted down to the white socks and canvas tennies on her feet. She dressed for comfort, as she did every day at *The Inquisitor*. But for some reason, she wished that she had taken the time to choose a more attractive outfit before coming in to work or had made the effort to put on some makeup.

She pressed the oversize jumper tight against her body, molding it to her slender figure. There was nothing about her figure that would be very appealing to a member of the opposite sex, nothing that would cause a man like Matt Garrison to look twice.

She had a pleasing shape, though nearly all of her features were rather ordinary and unimpressive. Her breasts were small, but not too small. Her legs were long, but not too long. All things considered, she was hopelessly average, living in a city where average meant a girl was out of the race before she even stepped up to the starting line.

But she was a writer, not some struggling model or hopeful starlet. What did she need with looks? Crafting a sentence was ten times more satisfying than having a man drool over her body, she rationalized, running her fingers through her tangled hair and replacing her glasses on her small but unpert nose. She had no need for that kind of attention. The solitude and the independence of a writing life were enough.

"That Matt Garrison is one gorgeous hunk of man." Casey glanced up to see Billie Jean Hopkins, *The Inquisitor's* resident Elvis expert, peeking over the top of the wall that separated their cubicles. Her voice was low and breathy and steeped in a southern accent. "He's enough to set a girl's insides on fire. Reminds me of The King, the way his hair falls across his forehead like that." B.J. had come to *The Inquisitor* from the mountains of northern Georgia, via Graceland. A lanky, dark-haired rebel firecracker, she and Casey had formed a friendship of sorts. Once a week during lunch they commiserated over the lack of eligible men in the state of California.

"I wouldn't know," Casey replied with a tight smile. In B.J.'s imagination, even Art Griswold had once resembled Elvis.

B.J. looked over at her and smiled. "No, I guess you wouldn't, would you? Tell me again, how long has it been since you've been on a date, honey?"

"What does that have to do with anything?" Casey asked.

"Nothin', 'cept I think Matt Garrison's got the hots for you. He's been askin' after you. If I didn't know better, I'd think there was something goin' on. He seemed awfully interested in learning everything he could about our darlin' Casey."

"What did you tell him?"

"I told him you prefer skinny blond men with long noses and clammy hands and that you haven't had a real date for two years."

Casey gasped. "You didn't!"

B.J. smiled slyly. "Of course I didn't, hon! I was just teasin'."

Casey's heart settled back into a normal rhythm. It had been over a year since she'd dated the man B.J. so fondly remembered as "Larry the Lizard," a brilliant software designer. He had been an experiment, a timeout from the models slash actors slash waiters she had dated since moving to L.A. But he had been no different, just another pretty face and shallow soul, another ex-boyfriend she had added to her list of species well below humans on the evolutionary scale.

It wouldn't do for Matt Garrison to know what a failure she was when it came to men. That would give him an advantage. He'd try to use his charm and good looks to seduce her into giving up on her story. Poor old spinster Casey Carmichael. Of course she'd fall head over heels for a guy like Matt.

Or at least that's what he'd assume. The fact that she knew his *modus operandi* could turn the situation to her advantage. And what did it matter what Matt Garrison thought about her, anyway?

"So, honey, you just say the word and I'll stay away."

Casey looked at B.J. "The word?"

"I'm not the kind of girl to horn in on another girl's territory. If you and Matt have somethin' goin', I'll keep my distance."

Casey laughed. "Garrison and me? You have got to be kidding. I wouldn't get within a mile of that snake if I could help it. He's all yours. Just keep him out of my hair."

B.J. smiled. "I'll do my best, hon. You can count on that." She waved coyly over the wall and walked out of the room, softly humming "Don't Be Cruel."

For an instant, Casey regretted her suggestion to B.J. With a sniff of annoyance, she stifled a tiny pinprick of jealousy and focused her mind on the bonus, on her dream.

A brass-framed photo on her desk caught her eye and she gazed at it longingly. The colors had faded slightly over the years, but she knew each detail of the scene by heart. A skinny girl with bright red hair stood between a white-haired couple. The man held a fishing pole in one hand and the little girl's hand in the other. The woman's arm was draped around the little girl's shoulders and the girl held a stringer of fish out to the camera, her face beaming with pride.

In the blurred background of the photo, a tiny cabin was visible. Tinier still was the window with the pink dotted Swiss curtains. She had grown up in that room in her grandparents' cabin. She had been safe and happy there and she would be happy there again.

She brushed an imaginary speck of dust from the glass, then ran her slender fingers lovingly over the top of the frame. Whenever she was discouraged by her life in L.A. or frustrated because of her lack of literary success, the picture was there to pull her through. "Never let go of your dreams," her grandfather had told her. "Dreams are what make life worth living." And then he would shake his head and tears would swim in the corners of his eyes. "Not like your mama. She let go of her dreams and look what happened to her."

Casey wasn't about to let go of her dreams. And she wasn't going to let Matt Garrison steal them from her, either.

She gathered her files on the Harrington case and put them in her bag. After a brief consideration, she picked up her trash can and sifted through the contents, picked out several pieces of paper and locked them in her desk drawer. She pocketed the key and was getting up to leave when the sound of Matt's voice outside the door to the office stopped her. Casey groaned inwardly. Why hadn't she left when she could?

She heard the sound of footsteps coming nearer and without a moment's hesitation, she shoved her chair back, bent down and crouched behind her desk. She could say she had dropped her pen. She reached over the edge of the desk and grabbed a pen for good measure. The sound of footsteps ceased and she waited a long minute before straightening up.

"I thought you'd jumped ship."

Casey jerked her head up and bumped her head on the front of her desk. With an irritated "Ouch," she looked up to find Matt Garrison watching her, his arms crossed over the edge of the cubicle and his chin resting on his fists.

"Drowning doesn't seem like a bad alternative when faced with the prospect of spending an evening with you," she muttered, rubbing her head and sliding back into her chair.

"Come on, Carmichael. Art told us to play nice."

"It's impossible to play nice with a rattlesnake. And even more ridiculous to have dinner with one." Casey pulled her wallet out of her bag and took out a ten-dollar bill. "Here, this is enough to buy you dinner at the Burger Barn. Let's just call it a night right now, before we do each other any physical harm."

"Art promised me a home-cooked meal," Matt replied. "I'm not leaving your side until I get one, Carmichael."

Casey glared at him, her lips stiffening into a straight line. She snatched a piece of paper from her desk and scribbled down her address. "I'm only doing this as a favor to Art. Seven o'clock. And be on time. I don't want to spend a minute more with you than I have to.

We'll just consider it a going-away party. After to-night, you're *going* to stay *away* from me. Got it?"

Matt gave her a charming smile before sauntering out of the room. "Whatever you say. . .darlin'."

"CAN I GIVE YOU a hand . . . Casey?"

Flinging the refrigerator door open, Casey bent down and pretended to search for some unneeded item. The cool rush of air from the open door felt good against her flushed face. Matt had arrived ten minutes before, and since then he had hovered over her like an impatient vulture, waiting for an opportune moment to descend. He wasn't wasting any time, Casey thought. Having him in her apartment was going to be worse than she thought.

She shoved a can of beer into his hand. "There's a Lakers game on television. Why don't you go watch it?" Casey turned back to her dinner preparations, and sighed with relief when the sound of the television drifted in from the living room moments later.

She inhaled deeply. Though he had left the room, the scent of his spicy cologne and his leather jacket remained, an indescribably male smell, foreign and almost exotic. In her mind, she saw Matt's smile, felt his eyes on her face. She imagined the feel of his beard-roughened cheek against her tingling fingertips, the feel of his hard mouth and eager tongue teasing at her—

The knife she was using to slice mushrooms slipped slightly, piercing the soft pad of her index finger. With a shout of pain, she dropped the offending utensil and rushed to the sink to staunch the flow of blood, in-

wardly scolding herself for her clumsiness and her per-
fidious thoughts.

"Are you all right?"

Casey could sense his presence behind her before he
spoke. His wide chest brushed against her back as he
peered over her shoulder. He reached around her,
grabbed her hand and pulled it out from under the icy
water. His breath was warm against the curve of her
neck and she closed her eyes at the rush of sensation that
swept from her toes to her fingertips. Very gently, he
turned her palm from side to side, his long fingers
splayed across the back of her hand. When his thumbs
dropped to her wrist, she wondered if he could feel her
racing pulse, if he knew what his touch was doing to
her.

That thought jerked her back to reality as quickly as
if someone had tossed ice water into her face. She
snatched her hand away, reached for a paper towel and
efficiently wrapped her finger, then slid her body along
the counter out of his encompassing warmth.

"I'm fine," she snapped. "Just a little cut." Casey
picked up the knife and attempted to finish slicing the
mushrooms, but the wad of paper towel on her finger
made the job nearly impossible.

"Here, let me." He was behind her again, this time to
pry the knife from her stiff fingers. She stepped aside,
moved across the kitchen and stood watching the play
of muscle across his back as he worked at the mundane
task.

"I once worked as a cook on a fishing boat off the
coast of Alaska," he began. Casey thought she heard a
slight hesitation in his softly spoken words, as if he was

uncertain about speaking to her. His voice had lost its cocky, challenging tone. "I learned to slice and dice in twenty-foot seas with pots and pans flying through the galley and hungry fishermen standing over my shoulder. Where do you want these?"

He turned to look at her, his hands in front of him, his fingers spread, and she stared at him blankly, trying to fathom what he was asking her. Where did she want his hands?

"What?"

"The mushrooms. Where do you want them?"

Casey felt a small stab of disappointment. "Oh, the mushrooms. Put them in that sauté pan with some butter."

He smiled and turned away. "What did you think I meant?" he asked.

"Nothing. Nothing at all. I wasn't paying attention."

"You do look a little pale. Maybe it's from all that blood you lost. You're lucky I came in here when I did. I probably saved your life. That makes twice in one day."

"Don't be ridiculous. It was a tiny little cut. I don't need any white knights riding to my rescue, thank you very much. I'm perfectly capable of saving my own life." Once out of her mouth, her words seemed stinging and shrewish and she wished that she could take them back.

"No, I guess you don't," he answered. A silence descended around them as he continued to stir the mushrooms and she continued to stare at his back. After several minutes, she broke the uncomfortable quiet.

"I can finish now. My finger has stopped bleeding."

"It's all right," he answered softly. "I'd like to help."

Casey gave him a guarded look then nodded. "All right. Take the mushrooms out of the pan, then add a little more butter." She took skinned and deboned chicken breasts out of the refrigerator, then stood beside him at the counter, tossing them with flour and spices in a plastic bag.

"What are we making?" he asked. When she looked up at him and smiled tentatively, he responded with a smile of his own.

"We are making chicken Carmichael, a variation on veal Marsala."

She sensed his eyes on her as he watched her work. Standing next to him, she felt the heat from his body and was tempted to take a tiny step closer to him, to brush up against his arm.

"Do you have any paprika?" His voice interrupted her thoughts.

"Chicken Carmichael does not call for paprika."

"It might be good, though. I had this dish in Yugoslavia once that had chicken and paprika and sweet wine in it and it was wonderful."

"I'm sure it was, but this dish doesn't have paprika in it."

"Oh, come on. Take a chance. Be adventurous," he teased. "Eating is one of life's great adventures. I ate blowfish in Japan and lived to tell the tale. And when I was in New Guinea, I ate fat white grubs and big black ants. Compared to that, a little paprika seems pretty tame, doesn't it?"

Casey turned to face him, a flour-covered piece of chicken dangling from her fingers. She should have known their momentary truce wouldn't last. Of all the arrogant, pushy— What was he implying? Did he think she was dull and boring?

"Listen, Garrison, this is my kitchen and I'm the cook here. If this dish were called chicken Garrison, then I'd add paprika and toss in a few ants and grubs for flavor. But this," she shouted, holding the chicken under his nose, "is chicken Carmichael and I prefer my chicken on the less adventurous side." She threw the chicken into the pan with enough force to spatter hot butter across the front of his shirt. "Just go back to your ball game while I finish dinner. This kitchen isn't big enough for the two of us."

As Matt left the room, Casey scolded herself silently. She had to admit she enjoyed the heat that Matt generated deep within her and the light that flickered in his eyes when he glanced her way. And they had embarked on a truce of sorts. But she must never forget that he was capable of reducing her dreams to ashes. Even so, she still felt inexplicably drawn to him.

"Like a moth to the flame," she muttered to herself as she flipped off the burner.

FIFTEEN MINUTES LATER, they sat across from each other at the small dining room table. Matt looked at Casey, trying to catch her eye, but she seemed preoccupied with her meal. The tension between them hummed in the silence, and Matt shifted uncomfortably in his chair.

He glanced around the apartment then back at the dinner table. A scene of suffocating domesticity, he thought. Yet, he was enjoying himself. Instead of feeling trapped as he normally did in such a situation, he felt comfortable in Casey's home, at Casey's table. Even though she hadn't said a word to him in the past ten minutes.

It didn't matter. Silence with Casey Carmichael was a helluva lot more stimulating than the sparkling conversation he had had with many other women.

He wondered what it would be like to sit across the dinner table from Casey every night. The adjectives "boring" and "stifling" didn't come to mind. He allowed his thoughts to drift to after-dinner activities, particularly those that would take place in the bedroom. God, what he wouldn't give to drag her into the bedroom and find out what was really behind that dagger-filled gaze and beneath that baggy dress she wore. A one-night stand with Casey Carmichael might be exactly what the doctor ordered. But somehow, the idea of waking up with her every morning and making love to her every night was much more intriguing.

Matt took a long sip of his beer. He knew exactly where this train of thought had come from—from Steve, Steve's new wife, and their newborn son. Steve Gordon was the closest thing he had to a best friend. As fellow photojournalists, they had shared some wild times together. Steve was a guy he could depend on, a guy who would put him up whenever he was in L.A. But when Matt had stopped at his apartment earlier that afternoon, Steve hadn't answered the door—his wife had.

Matt hadn't seen the guy in nearly two years, hadn't talked to him, hadn't written. And in that time, Steve had found a woman, gotten married, and started a family.

At first, Matt had felt irritated that his friend would give up his freedom for the confines of marriage. Then he felt guilty that he had let their friendship lapse for such a long time. And as the front door closed on Steve's happy life, envy burrowed its way into his mind.

The unsatisfied feeling that used to keep him searching for bigger and better adventures now had him thinking about settling down, finding a place to call home, developing friendships that lasted longer than the length of a photo assignment. The distance he maintained in all of his relationships was a survival mechanism. His freedom was more important than the people who drifted in and out of his life. Without freedom, his life as he knew it would come to an end; his career would fall into a deep, dark chasm of responsibility.

Matt knew that wishing for the best of both worlds was a waste of time. If he could afford to make friends, Casey would be the first person he would choose. She was smart and resourceful and if he could allow himself to fall in love with anyone, she would probably be at the top of his list.

Casey saw him as he really was, and though the picture wasn't very flattering, at least he didn't have to live up to any preconceived expectations. He could be himself around her. Mutual distrust appeared to be a much better way to start a relationship with a woman than unbridled lust.

Matt set his beer down and smiled. "You look very nice tonight," he said, hoping to break the icy wall that split the dining room table.

Casey looked up at him, a cautious glint in her green eyes. "What is that supposed to mean?"

He was surprised by her reaction to his compliment. "Exactly what I said."

She gazed levelly at him. "Your charm isn't going to work on me, Garrison," she said, a satisfied smile curling her lips. "I know exactly what's behind that pretty face. I know your kind."

A familiar uneasiness came over him at the mention of his face. His father's face. Why couldn't he have been born with an ordinary face?

He remembered one particular incident in a bar in New Orleans and smiled at the memory. The guy was enormous and, fortunately, drunk as a skunk. In addition, he was extremely jealous of the attention his girlfriend had given Matt the moment he had walked in the door. The drunk had ended up sprawled unconscious on the floor and Matt had walked away needing ten stitches in his chin. He also walked away with the guy's girlfriend. He had hoped his picture-perfect face, the mirror image of his father's, had been ruined. But it seemed like the scar brought more attention to his looks, not less.

He'd fought hard at not becoming his father, a man whose life revolved around a mahogany-paneled office. He hadn't wanted to follow in his father's footsteps, so he had taken a minor talent for photography and turned it into a career. He'd begun with a hundred-dollar camera he'd picked up in a pawn shop and had snapped pictures of anything that seemed newsworthy. He was fearless and would go into any situation to get a good picture. He had sold his first photos—photos of a bank robber and his twelve hostages—to Art Griswold at *The Boston Globe*. When they'd appeared on the front page the next day with his own photo credit, he had waited for his father to call and congratulate him. The call had not come. But a tersely worded letter had, telling him to give up his "silly hobby" or give up his inheritance. It hadn't been a difficult choice.

Matt glanced back at Casey, but her interest had shifted to her water glass. He cleared his throat. So charm hadn't worked. Maybe honesty would. "Dinner was very good," he ventured. "Art was right. You'll make some man a wonderful wife someday."

*Damn, where had that comment come from? A wonderful wife?* It had seemed ridiculous when Art had said it. It seemed even more ridiculous coming out of his own mouth.

Without a word, Casey rose from the table and carried her plate into the kitchen. "I'm going to take a walk. Lock the door on your way out." Matt watched as she grabbed her jacket from the hall closet, pulled on her tennis shoes, and picked up her bag from the coffee table, then slammed the door behind her.

He looked down at his plate and stabbed angrily at a piece of chicken. Getting Casey Carmichael to trust him was going to be a lot harder than he had thought. Especially if he was going to walk around with his foot in his mouth.

THE APARTMENT WAS DARK when she returned. She would have stayed away longer, but the coffee shop down the street closed at eleven. The dog-eared notebook she carried contained the rough draft of the next scene of Theodora's latest adventure, so the evening hadn't been a total waste.

The fluorescent light from above the kitchen sink filtered into the living room, bathing the room in silver light and velvet shadow, and revealed a long form stretched out on the sofa. She wasn't surprised that he had stayed.

His breathing was slow and even and Casey listened for several moments as her eyes adjusted to the darkness. His shirt was unbuttoned and the light gleamed on the contours of his bare chest, diffused only by the sprinkling of hair that began at his collarbone and drifted down to end somewhere below the waistband of his jeans.

His face was hidden in darkness, but she could see his hair, rumpled by sleep. Her hands clenched convulsively as she thought about running her fingers through the silky strands. It was the color of mahogany, straight and thick and perpetually windblown. He looked as if he had stepped straight out of an ad for cigarettes or four-wheel-drive trucks or whiskey.

Gorgeous, that's what B.J. had called him. Casey remembered how his face had tightened at her own waspish remarks about his looks. What was it, embarrassment? Had her comments unnerved him? He had actually blushed. Maybe there was a chink in his gleaming armor after all.

Well, she had spoken the truth. He could try to ply his charms all he wanted and she wouldn't capitulate. She still had her ace safely in the hole. She was certain that Matt hadn't come across the plane ticket in Finkleman's hotel room. In fact, she'd bet money that he hadn't uncovered much of anything before they'd been tossed out of the Beverly Palms and that was probably the reason for his devoted interest in her. Casey felt a small stab of disappointment. But what if he was interested in her for another reason? How would she feel then?

*Don't be a fool, Casey Carmichael! He's interested in one thing and one thing only. Your story!*

She watched him a moment more, then turned away.

"How's your finger?" The sound of his voice didn't startle her; she had been secretly longing for him to speak.

She turned back to him and smiled hesitantly. "It's all right. Why are you still here?"

She watched as he sat up and her eyes were drawn to his bare chest and rippled abdomen. He pulled his shirt closed, buttoning it quickly, then stretched to reach the lamp on the end table. Light flooded the room, and Casey squinted against the sudden glare.

"I've been waiting for you to come home." He patted the place beside him on the couch. "Sit down. I think you and I need to talk."

Casey sat down on the far end of the couch and tucked her legs underneath her. Pulling off her glasses, she rubbed her tired eyes then looked over at him.

"I hope you don't plan on setting up camp here," she said. Her voice was strained and the statement sounded more like a thinly-veiled invitation to leave.

"To be honest, I could use a place to stay tonight. There's a guy I usually stay with but he's ... out of town...on business." He hesitated, considering his next words, then plunged ahead. "Listen, Carmichael, I think you and I should come to some sort of understanding about this story."

"Why is it so important to you? Why can't you just drop it?"

He looked at her in surprise, as if she had just asked him to "drop" breathing. "Twenty-five thousand dollars is a lot to give up. I need the money."

"For what?"

"For plane tickets and food. Do you know how long I could live on that kind of money? For at least a year, maybe two or three. I know a guy who's funding an expedition to the Chilean Andes in February. He told me I could come along and photograph the trip, but right now I don't have the money for a plane ticket to San Diego, much less Santiago."

"Well, I need the money just as much as you do."

"For what?"

"For—" Casey hesitated. "For something very important. For something I've wanted for a very long time." An image of her childhood home drifted through her thoughts.

"And you won't reconsider working on this story with me? I could get to Chile on half the money. What about you? Couldn't you be satisfied with half the pie?"

Casey sighed. She was tempted to agree to his plan, but there were too many warning bells that sounded when she thought about working with Matt Garrison. She wasn't sure she could trust him. Would he really be satisfied with half the money or was that just a ploy to gain her confidence? And being in close proximity to him would be difficult. Matt Garrison was a dangerous man and she was dangerously close to losing her self-control.

*Don't trust him, Casey.*

*Aw, come on, Casey! Take a chance. You only live once.*

*Don't give in. Remember your dream. Remember. Remember.*

"All right. Fine," she said, throwing up her hands. "You win. We can work together on this, but if you don't pull your own weight, Garrison, I'm dumping you the first chance I get."

A boyish smile broke across his face. "Great! When do we start?"

Casey felt a wave of guilt at her next words. She wondered if her face telegraphed the bald-faced lie she was about to tell. "I have some loose ends to tie up on another story. Why don't we meet for dinner on Friday night. Six o'clock at Ernie's Grill. We can go over what we both have and put together a plan." His expression remained the same—bright and satisfied. He hadn't detected anything unusual in her appearance. Maybe lying got easier with practice, she thought.

Suddenly, without warning, he slid across the couch and took her hands in his. Looking into her eyes, he lowered his head. Her heart began to race and she was tempted to pull away, but she wanted him to kiss her, to rekindle the fire she had felt earlier that day in Finkleman's hotel room.

At the last moment, he turned his face and his warm lips came to rest on her cheek. It was a quiet, friendly, undemanding kiss. When he drew his head back, he smiled at her candidly. "We'll make a great team, Carmichael."

"Why did you do that?"

"Kiss you?"

Casey nodded her head.

He shrugged his shoulders. "To seal the deal. If we're going to work together we might as well be friends."

Casey stood up nervously, putting space between them. He was staring at her now, a distant look on his face and an uneasy smile on his lips.

She sighed. "All right, you can spend the night on my couch. But I'm warning you, my bedroom door will be locked, so don't even consider any funny business." Casey rubbed her forehead distractedly, wondering if she had just made a huge error in judgment. "It's late. I'm going to bed. I want you gone before I get up tomorrow morning." She started for the bedroom, but his voice stopped her.

"Carmichael?"

"Yes, Garrison?" She didn't turn around.

"See you Friday night. Six o'clock sharp."

Casey was glad he couldn't see her face, for this time her expression would have given her away. She wouldn't be at Ernie's Grill on Friday night; she'd be on a plane to Denver, on the trail of Emily Harrington and the wedding of the year. And Matt Garrison would be exactly where she wanted him. As far away from *her* story as possible.

## 3

*The 727 was taxiing to the runway when I noticed the man in the seat across the aisle. He wore a trench coat, belted tightly at the waist, a brown fedora pulled low over his eyes, and black leather gloves. In most situations, this wouldn't cause the slightest bit of curiosity, but it had been close to one hundred degrees in the shade when we boarded the plane at LAX. It didn't take the full power of my highly developed deductive reasoning to know this was the guy who had been tailing me all week. The seat next to him was empty. I stood up, crossed the aisle and sat down. As far as I was concerned, neither one of us would be leaving this plane until I knew exactly what he wanted.*

CASEY GLANCED UP from her notebook and noticed the flight attendants beginning their preparations for takeoff. Her stomach tightened with uncontrollable panic. The long-forgotten feeling was back, this time in an adult-strength dosage, and she wondered if she would make it through the flight without being sick to her stomach.

It was now or never, she thought grimly. *If I don't get off now, I'm going to be trapped on this plane until it lands in Denver.*

But she was determined to bury the overwhelming urge to run. She was an adult now, and the fears of childhood could be dealt with in a calm and reasonable manner. She leaned out into the aisle and tried to catch a glimpse of the passengers in first class, just seven rows in front of her. Emily Harrington was there, dressed inconspicuously in an oversize sweater and jeans. Dark glasses and a fashionably slouchy hat hid her eyes and hair from public view. No one had recognized her yet. The flight attendant was coming closer now and Casey wondered if her face looked as pale as she suspected it did.

"Could you put your tray table up, ma'am?" the woman asked with a bright smile. "We'll be leaving the gate in just a few minutes."

Casey hastily stuffed her notebook and pen into her carryon, flipped up the tray, and checked her seat belt for the umpteenth time. She noticed the airplane's safety manual in the pocket of the seat in front of her and she pulled it out and studied it carefully, noting the location of the emergency exits. She hadn't flown in over twenty years, not since that last harrowing summer visit with her mother when she was thirteen, but she could recite the safety litany word for word. "Your seat cushion will serve as a flotation device . . . in the event of a loss of cabin pressure . . . emergency exits located over each wing." Panic threatened to smother her again and she drew a deep breath, trying to subdue a feeling of nausea.

This wasn't going to work! She had to get off the plane now. Casey bent over and pulled on her bag, but it was wedged snugly underneath the seat.

She looked up to see the portly businessman in the window seat watching her, his porcine eyes surveying her body in undisguised appreciation. He smiled at her in encouragement. "I have to get off the plane," she whispered frantically. "I have to get off now." One final tug brought the bag sliding out from under the seat and Casey rose to make her way down the aisle.

"Lurleen? Honey, is that you?"

She felt her heart stop. No! It couldn't be! What was Garrison doing here?

Casey flopped back down in her seat without looking up and buried her face in her hands. How had he known where to find her? No one knew! He was supposed to be at Ernie's Grill waiting for her.

"Lurleen, darlin'." He was standing over her now. Casey jerked her head up and glared into his eyes. He returned her angry glare with a mocking smile. "Honey," he cooed, "I thought it was you. What are you doing out of the hospital? Last I heard, they was gonna keep you locked up for another year." Out of the corner of her eye Casey could see the businessman shift in his seat and press himself closer to the window as he stared at them in curiosity.

"You're the one," Casey said, the anger and tension in her voice barely controlled. "You've been following me, haven't you?" The uneasy feeling of being tailed had been with her since the morning Matt had left her apartment. She had written it off as her imagination, but now she knew exactly how he had come to be here. Casey groaned inwardly. He had probably followed her to the travel agency, walked in minutes after she walked out, and booked the same flight she had. She had led him right to Emily.

"Now, honey, don't be angry with me. It's me who should be mad." Matt lowered his voice and directed his next comments at her seatmate. "Lurleen has a mighty nasty temper. Few months back she got mad at me for just starin' at her. Doctor calls it paranoia. She imagines people are followin' her, too. I was just lookin' at her, ya know, just appreciatin' her feminine assets, and she takes off after me with this big old butcher knife. Stabbed me twice before I got the knife away from her." Matt yanked on his shirt. "Wanna see the scar?"

The businessman jumped from his seat and pushed past Casey. "No, thank you," he mumbled, his eyes darting back and forth nervously as he stumbled down the aisle looking for an available seat.

"Hey, mister, you can have 27F," Matt called after him, his voice cracking with humor. "That's my seat. I'll just sit here next to Lurleen." Matt hastily stowed his aluminum-frame backpack in the overhead compartment then pushed his way past Casey to the window seat and dropped his camera bag between them.

Casey stared straight ahead, refusing to acknowledge his presence. Garrison was here, on the plane, with her. But how much did he know? Maybe, if she was lucky, she could lose him in Denver. That was, if she made it through the flight.

"Don't even think about it," he warned.

"What are you talking about?"

"Your little mind is grinding away, trying to come up with some way of getting rid of me. Well, it's not going to work. We had a deal, Carmichael, and I intend to see that you don't back out of it."

She turned in her seat to face him, her eyes narrowed, her temper barely controlled. "A deal? A deal implies some exchange of goods and services. As I recall, you haven't offered anything in exchange for tagging along with me. Besides, this trip has nothing at all to do with our deal. I'm simply taking a vacation."

Matt leaned back in his seat and smiled. "I've been thinking about taking a vacation myself. And just what makes you think I don't have anything to offer?"

"All right, let's hear it," she challenged, her chin raised in defiance. "Come on, Garrison, tell me what you have."

"Ever heard the saying 'A picture is worth a thousand words'?" he asked. "The bonus is for a story plus photos."

"Any idiot can use a camera. Why would I need you?"

"In addition to offering my estimable talents as a photographer, I happen to know where we're going."

She smiled sarcastically. "How clever of you. All you needed for that incredibly common piece of knowledge was a good look at your own airline ticket. And how did you manage to buy an airline ticket? I thought you were broke. Or was that claim just for my benefit?"

"Griswold gave me an advance on our payment for the story," he said nonchalantly.

Casey's eyes widened. "He *what?* You had no right! The story is mine. You better start figuring a way to pay

Griswold back, because it's not coming from *my* bonus on this story."

"But you need me, Carmichael. I know where Emily's going."

"Emily?" Casey's heart fell and she tried to keep her surprise and disappointment from registering on her face. He knew Emily was on the plane.

"Emily Harrington. You know, the woman in first class with the hat and sunglasses. The subject of our story, Sherlock. And don't think I bought the vacation bit for one minute."

"She's going to Laramie," Casey admitted, certain that he already knew that fact.

"And where's she going from there? Movie stars like Emily Harrington don't spend their free time wandering around airports." Matt watched her, a self-satisfied grin curling his lips. "Don't tell me Casey Carmichael, investigative reporter *extraordinaire*, got on this plane without any idea of where she was headed? Rule number one, a good reporter—"

"Fine," she interrupted. "You win. Tell me, where are we going?"

Matt paused, then smiled broadly. "No," he answered, "I think I'll keep that little piece of information to myself. It'll keep you honest."

Casey opened her mouth to reply then suddenly realized the plane was moving. She felt the color drain from her face and could hear the blood rush through her veins. She squeezed her eyes closed, took a deep breath and leaned back in her seat. From a great distance, she heard the sound of a bell and the pilot's voice over the intercom. "Flight attendants, prepare for takeoff." In her preoccupation with Matt, she hadn't realized that the plane had moved out to the runway.

"Carmichael, are you all right? Geez, you look a little green."

"Shut up, Garrison," she said through clenched teeth. She felt the plane accelerate beneath her, the jet engines drowning out the roar of her heartbeat in her head. "I think I'm going to be sick," Casey moaned, her eyes still shut.

Matt's fingers slid through the hair at the nape of her neck, gently pushing her forward until her forehead came to rest on her knees.

"Breathe," his soothing voice urged. "Nice, deep breaths. Let your body relax. There's nothing to be frightened of. Flying is a perfectly safe means of travel."

Casey felt hot tears work their way to the corners of her eyes as she tried to control her nausea. How much more humiliation could she take? Was she doomed to be at her absolute worst whenever he was near?

"There. Did you feel that? We just left the ground. Now, the next ninety seconds are the scariest. Most plane crashes happen in the first ninety seconds of takeoff. If we don't crash during that time, odds are we won't." Matt's fingers continued to massage the back of her neck, working at the knotted cords of muscle.

"That makes me feel so much better," she muttered. Casey felt a thud from the underside of the plane. "Oh, Lord."

"That's just the landing gear coming up. Now, count it down. Ninety, eighty-nine, eighty-eight."

Casey took over the count, breathing deeply and trying to relax her body. Miraculously, by the time she reached "one" her nausea had disappeared. Slowly she raised her head and opened her eyes. The plane was in the air and for the first time in her life, she had gotten through a takeoff without getting sick all over her shoes. Matt was watching her with a look of concern.

"Okay now?" he asked with a reassuring smile. His fingers were still tangled in her hair, warm and gentle, and she shivered. "Is this the first time you've flown?"

Casey shook her head, but he kept his hand on the back of her neck. "No," she croaked. "I used to fly all the time when I was a kid. No matter how many times I flew, I was still terrified being alone on the plane with no control over what happened."

"My parents used to put me on a plane for military school every fall. At first I was scared to fly alone, but then I got used to it."

"You went to military school?" A wavering smile touched her lips. "I find that hard to believe."

"I was what they called 'incorrigible,'" he explained. "A real handful. When I wasn't actually in trouble, I was figuring out new ways of getting into trouble. I attended five of the country's finest military prep schools and got kicked out of all of them before my parents finally gave up."

"Now why doesn't *that* surprise me?"

"What about you?"

The gentle movement of his fingers on her nape had lulled her into a warm feeling of security. It seemed natural, talking to him about her past, opening up doors that had been closed for years. "Every summer, my grandparents would pack me off to see Louise wherever she happened to be." She smiled then tipped her head forward, relishing the touch of his fingers. "Louise was, or is, my mother." She turned slightly to look at him, but he didn't seem to find anything peculiar in what she was saying, so she continued. "I never wanted to go. I used to plead with Gram and Gramp to let me stay home with them, but I think they were afraid to break the connection. I was the only contact they had with their daughter."

"What about your father?"

The question was natural, casually asked, and she had answered it countless times as a child. She shrugged her shoulders, numb to the pain the inquiry should have caused. "I never knew my father. He disappeared before I was born."

For a moment Matt was taken aback, but then smoothly recovered. "Lucky girl," he said quietly. "There were times in my childhood when I would have thought that was good fortune."

At Casey's questioning gaze, he continued, his voice dry and cynical. "My father and I don't exactly see eye to eye. He's wealthy, powerful and has blood as blue as the Arctic Ocean and twice as cold. He and my mother coexist in Boston with my perfectly loyal and obedient younger brother and my dutiful but covertly rebellious younger sister. They have a typical society marriage. They haven't slept together in twenty-five years." Casey could hear an edge of pain in the offhand commentary.

"At least you have a family," she sighed wistfully. "I'd give anything for a real family. You know, a *Father Knows Best* family. A mom, a dad, a brother, a sister. I used to dream about it at night when I was a kid."

"What about your grandparents? Aren't they family?"

"They both passed away fourteen years ago when I was nineteen. I've been al—" Casey paused to rephrase her thoughts "—on my own since then."

"You and I have something in common then. I've been on my own since I was eighteen. What about your mom?"

"I got a Christmas card from her the year before Gram and Gramp died. That's the last time I heard from her. I have no idea where she is. My mother calls herself a Gypsy soul. She used to say, 'Casey, your mama's just got a vagabond heart. Wandering's the only thing I'm good at.' She was right," Casey said with a smile. "She tried hard, but she was a horrible mother."

She had learned long ago to accept her mother for the person she was. Not every woman was cut out to be a mom. Casey had just had the unfortunate luck of ending up with one who hadn't even come close. She would do things much differently, she mused. When she had children, she would be there for them. . . .

Matt's voice interrupted her uncurbed thoughts. "She couldn't have been too bad. You turned out pretty well."

Casey smiled uncomfortably at him. "My grandparents raised me from the time I was a baby," she replied softly, her voice breaking slightly. "They deserve the credit."

They sat in companionable silence for several minutes. The walls she had so carefully constructed to protect herself from his charms had disappeared and she found herself feeling at ease in his presence. Maybe she could get along with him. Maybe working together could be bearable. But could she trust him?

"Why don't you close your eyes and try to sleep," he said softly. "We should be in Denver in a couple of hours."

He pulled his hand away from her neck and tipped up the armrests between them, to give her room to relax. Casey leaned back in her seat, silently wishing that he would put his hand back on her neck. She twisted slightly, then closed her eyes, but it was impossible to get comfortable. Then, she felt Matt's arm slide around her shoulders and she opened her eyes in surprise.

He smiled down at her. "You can use my shoulder for a pillow," he explained. "Now be a good girl and close your eyes."

"Thanks," Casey murmured before drifting off to sleep.

"CAN I GET A PILLOW for your wife, sir?"

Matt looked up at the pretty blond flight attendant who stood in the aisle. She had passed his seat several times in the last ten minutes, and each time had given him a dazzling smile. Not one of those may-I-help-you smiles, but a smile that signaled a definite interest.

He looked over at Casey and grinned. "She's not my wife."

The woman's smile intensified. "Your fiancée?"

"No. And not my girlfriend or my sister. Just a business associate." He took the lure and gave her a suggestive look.

He saw a spark of delight in the woman's eyes and she bent down a little closer. "Is there anything I can get for you? Coffee, soda, a drink, maybe?"

Matt opened his mouth, ready with a remark laced with sexual innuendo. The words that escaped his lips surprised him as much as they surprised her. "A little peace and quiet would be nice," he answered, leaning back and closing his eyes. "Maybe you could ask the captain to turn off the engines for a little while?"

He heard an uncomfortable giggle before she moved away. A few days ago he would have played the game, teasing and flirting, conversing in sentences dripping with verbal foreplay. Some of his best conquests had started and ended on airplanes. He was a charter member of the "Mile High Club." But suddenly, the game held no appeal.

Matt turned slightly and drew in a deep breath, inhaling the pleasant scent of Casey's hair. The soft strands tickled his chin and he bent his head to look at her face. Her cheek was pressed against his chest and her hand clutched the front of his shirt, her fingers stiff, as if they held her fear of flying in reserve until she woke up.

What was it about Casey Carmichael that poked at the dying embers of his honor? She wasn't what most men would consider beautiful. She was stubborn and impertinent and a genuine pain in the rear, qualities that most men would find unpalatable. And she wasn't even remotely attracted to him. Maybe that was it. She presented a challenge he had never confronted before. A woman whose entire being was impervious to his looks and charms.

But there was more to it than that, he thought to himself. He felt good just sitting next to her. He enjoyed listening to the musical sound of her voice, watching her green eyes flash in anger, seeing her battle her fears and overcome them. Just being with her was enough.

Yes, she was sweet, but she was also standing in the way of his twenty-five thousand dollars—an inconvenient yet alluring roadblock.

Matt thought back to the kiss they had shared in the hotel room, the sweet taste of her mouth, the tentative touch of her tongue. He felt a warm rush of blood course through him and collect in the vicinity of his lap. Drawing her limp form closer within the circle of his arm, he let his hand move down her shoulder to her rib cage, his fingers sliding beneath the soft underside of her breast. Though her clothing was a barrier between his fingers and her flesh, he could feel the warm weight of her. He fought the urge to let his hand explore farther.

Right. Just being with her might be enough for now, but how long would that last? How long would it be before he wanted more? Casey was not the type of woman to engage in a casual relationship and that was all he could afford to give her. He couldn't allow any attachments. No relationships meant no problems. He moved his hand back to her shoulder. The whole issue was a moot point, anyway. Once he scooped her on the story, he'd be the last person she'd want around.

Still, there was something more going on between him and Casey Carmichael. Something more than merely a bothersome sexual attraction. He just wasn't quite sure what it was.

"CASEY?" SHE HEARD the gentle voice calling to her through the darkness. "Honey, wake up." But she was so warm, so safe. She snuggled closer to the source of the warmth, a tiny moan of protest escaping her lips. "Casey, open those pretty eyes of yours. We're on the ground."

Casey smiled and drifted toward consciousness. That voice. So incredibly smooth and deep. She could drown in that voice as it washed over her in waves of softly spoken endearments.

Warm hands grasped her shoulders and she let the hands pull her forward, anticipating the feel of a muscular chest beneath her fingertips, the heat of a hard body as it covered the length of hers. Instead, the hands began to shake her and the deep voice was loud and insistent. "Come on, Carmichael, rise and shine."

Casey slowly opened her eyes and squinted into the electric gleam of Matt Garrison's smile. She opened her mouth, intending to demand that he cease his abuse, but all she could manage was a louder, more insistent groan.

"Wake up, Sherlock. We have to get off the plane."

"A-a-all r-r-right," she said, her voice catching on every shake. "I—I—I'm awake." He looked into her eyes for several spellbinding moments before he gave her one last playful shake. Casey pulled her eyes away reluctantly and looked around. The plane was empty.

"Emily!" she said, coming fully awake. "Why didn't you wake me sooner? We have to follow Emily."

"That would have been a little bit difficult with you tossed over my shoulder like a snoring sack of flour. I'd rather not call too much attention to ourselves. It's best if we board at the last minute."

Casey stood up so hurriedly that her head almost collided with the overhead compartment. She heard Matt suck in his breath and glanced over to see a hint of worry cross his perfect features. Then, he shook his head, the worry replaced by a look of relief.

"What?" she asked blandly.

"The longer I know you, Carmichael, the more amazed I am that you've managed to live to the ripe old age of thirty-three."

Casey bent down to pull her bag out from under the seat and grazed her forehead on the back of the seat in front of her. "Thirty-three is not old," she muttered.

"It is to a twenty-five-year-old."

*Oh, please,* she thought to herself. He's twenty-five? I've been fantasizing about a man eight years younger than me!

Casey was afraid to look up at him, afraid he would see the shock on her face. "Twenty-five?" she said, her voice choking slightly. "I would have thought you were older. You seem more . . . worldly."

She could sense him smiling at her now. "I am," he answered. She fumbled with her ticket as she straightened up, hoping to hide her expression of pleasure. So he *was* older.

"More worldly, that is," he added, his voice serious. She risked a look up at him and saw a teasing grin break across his face. "And older by another ten years."

Lord, the man could be irritating! He seemed to delight in making her look like a fool.

Casey stepped out into the aisle, anxious to put some distance between them before she lost her temper, but he followed closely behind, nudging her backside with the corner of his bag. When she turned to complain, he was still grinning.

"Had you worried for a second, didn't I?"

The airport was crowded; every gate overflowed with passengers, many dressed in colorful ski jackets, some wearing cowboy hats. As they walked down the concourse, she saw a number of people curled up on the floor in the waiting area, asleep.

"Damn," Matt growled.

"What's wrong?"

"Take a look out the window, Carmichael. It's snowing pretty hard out there. Half the people in this airport are probably stranded here, waiting for the snow to let up."

"So?"

"So let's hope our plane gets off the ground." Matt stopped for a moment to stare up at a bank of monitors, then continued his brisk pace down the concourse. "It looks like most of the flights going west into the ski resorts are cancelled. We're headed north. Maybe we'll beat it. Gate A-16. That's at the other end of the airport. Come on, we'd better hurry." Casey picked up her pace, afraid she might lose him in the crush of travelers. Her small suitcase felt as if it was loaded with lead and her shoulder bag kept sliding down, pulling her to a stop every fifty yards. She kept her eyes on Matt's huge red backpack and wondered how he could weave in and out among people with such ease. He was obviously used to navigating through airports.

She lost him somewhere near Concourse B but found him waiting for her anxiously when she arrived at the gate, flushed and out of breath.

"Thought I lost you for a minute there, Sherlock."

Casey smiled caustically, then threw herself into a chair and dropped her bags at her feet. "Anyone who claims chivalry is not dead never met you," she muttered.

"No time to rest," he said, grabbing her elbow and dragging her up. "Come on, the plane's boarding."

Casey picked up her bags and followed him reluctantly to the gate. She felt a growing sense of dread and tried to ignore it. Another plane. Another takeoff. And another opportunity to humiliate herself in front of Garrison. But she was an experienced flyer now, she told herself. She had gotten through the first flight; she could get through this one.

She and Matt followed a pair of passengers through the doorway labeled A-16. But instead of walking through a long jetway, they went down a short hallway. At the end, a cold gust of air slapped her in the face, and she realized they were going outside. But why?

Casey learned the reason the moment she stepped into the blowing snow. Fifty feet in front of her, barely visible through the swirling blanket of white, was the plane. A tiny two-engine propeller plane with a rickety metal staircase pushed up to the door. She stared, openmouthed, watching the icy wind buffet the narrow wings of the plane, and counted seven windows along its length.

"No!" she shouted, paralyzed with fear, her feet frozen to the ground.

Matt turned around, then noticed she had stopped following him. He hurried back, grabbed her bag and shouted at her over the sputtering of the plane's engines. "Come on, Carmichael. You'll be fine."

"No!" she repeated, more firmly this time. "I'm not getting on that plane."

"What do you mean? Are you crazy?" he yelled. "Get on the plane!"

Casey winced at the anger in his voice. She couldn't. This time it was much more than the prospect of being humiliated again. It was pure, unadulterated fear. "I can't," she shouted, her mouth close to Matt's ear. "I just can't. Please, let's rent a car and drive to Laramie. It won't take that long," she begged, hoping he would understand and praying that Laramie was a driveable distance from Denver.

For a moment, she thought she saw understanding and concern in his eyes. He opened his mouth as if to acquiesce, but then closed it, shook his head and tossed her bag into the snow at her feet.

"I'm getting on that plane, Carmichael, whether you do or not," he said as he turned and walked away from her. She watched in disbelief as he mounted the steps to the plane, silently hoping he would turn around and make his way back to her. The tentative trust that had developed between them had vanished in the blink of an eye. After everything he had done to help her through the first flight, he was deserting her.

"Garrison, get back here," she shouted through the hiss of the driving snow and the whine of the spinning propellers. But he didn't hear her. He just kept climbing.

At the last moment, he looked over his shoulder and gave her a jaunty salute. Though she couldn't read his expression through the blinding snow, she could picture the self-satisfied smirk on his face, the knowing look in his eyes.

The wind cut through her jacket and she shivered uncontrollably. Her eyes began to water from the cold and she could feel an angry tear trickle from the corner of her eye to freeze on her cheek.

Damn him! Damn his arrogant, two-faced soul. He had deserted her. He'd managed to snatch her story right out from under her. And, to top it all off, she had helped him right along.

Casey spun around angrily and walked back inside the terminal. The distance seemed agonizingly long as her mind ran through the ramifications of her decision not to board the plane. He knew where Emily was staying. She didn't. He was on his way to Laramie. She wasn't.

With a dejected sigh, Casey sat down in a deserted corner of the waiting area, battling tears of frustration and self-disgust. She didn't deserve to get the story. Garrison was right. She didn't have the experience or the brains.

With hesitant fingers, she drew an envelope from her shoulder bag and pulled out a tattered and creased letter.

Dear Miss Carmichael,

I am happy to inform you that your offer to buy your grandparents' home has been accepted by the current owners. Enclosed are the final papers for you to sign with the sale contingent on approval of financing.

I have put in a good word for you at the bank and I don't believe you'll have any problem getting a loan. The loan officer tells me that you'll need approximately $5,000 to close the deal. Within the next week he will be forwarding the loan papers for you to complete.

I know how difficult it was for you when you were forced to sell your grandparents' home for back taxes. I'm glad I was of some assistance in bringing the granddaughter of my old friends, Harold and Marjorie Carmichael, back to the old Carmichael place.

Sincerely,
John L. Hughes
Attorney at Law

Five thousand dollars. The price of her dream. Three days ago she had wanted the entire bonus. A few hours ago she had been willing to compromise on half. Now she would have to settle for nothing. In a single moment of supremely childish cowardice, she had let her dream slip through her fingers. Garrison had won.

Casey buried her face in her hands. Damn his treacherous soul! He was on his way to Laramie and she wasn't....

But she *could* be.

Casey snatched her wallet from her bag and quickly thumbed through the bills jammed inside. She wasn't finished yet, not by a long shot. She could rent a car and drive to Laramie. Three years in L.A. had done nothing for her winter driving skills, but maybe with luck, the snow would clear by morning.

She could call the Laramie airport and try to persuade some greedy ticket agent to watch for Emily and let her know where she was going. Or better yet, she could have someone watch for Garrison. He'd probably wait until the next day to track Emily down, giving Casey extra time to track him down.

She smiled to herself in growing excitement. All was not lost.

After mentally adding the cost of a rental car and the cost of a possible bribe or two, she realized she was running dangerously low on cash. Her travel advance from *The Inquisitor* was nearly gone. She had a personal credit card, but using that was like gambling with borrowed money. But desperate times called for desperate measures.

A hotel room for the night was out of the question. She would have to catch some sleep in the airport and leave first thing in the morning.

Casey's pace was more upbeat as she hurried back through the concourse. First she would find a snitch to watch for Garrison. Matt would be landing in Laramie in an hour, so she didn't have much time. Then maybe she could turn the unused portion of her plane ticket in for cash. After that, she would get a quick bite to eat and a few hours' sleep.

The cat-and-mouse game she was playing with Matt Garrison wasn't over yet.

# 4

*I knew he was behind me before he spoke. Whenever he was near, the air seemed to be charged with a kind of erotic electricity. He touched me on the shoulder and I felt the current rush through me. Even though he was a two-faced snake in the grass, he still had the power to set my senses on fire. I turned slowly and leveled the barrel of my .38 revolver at his chest, the gun cocked and ready to fire. He didn't blink, didn't even flinch. He just smiled that three-hundred-watt smile of his. "You don't really want to shoot me, do you, Theo." It was a statement, not a question. But he was wrong. At that precise moment in time, he was dead . . .*

"WHAT ARE YOU WRITING?"

Casey froze, her pen suspended above her notebook. With deliberately precise movements, she closed it, arranged her pen neatly on top, and took a deep breath. Swiveling slowly on the lunch-counter stool, she tried to calm the racing of her heart, an erratic rhythm that had begun the instant she heard his voice.

He was standing over her, a teasing grin curving the corners of his mouth. She looked up at him, her feelings a mixture of suspicion and relief. "What are you doing here? I thought you were on your way to Laramie."

Matt slid onto the empty stool beside her and picked at the leftover french fries on her plate. "Me? Get on a plane and leave my partner behind? Now why would I even think of doing something as *conniving*...and *deceitful*...and *disloyal* as that?" he asked, his voice laced with sarcasm.

Blushing, Casey turned her back on him and casually sipped her coffee. "Your flight was cancelled, wasn't it?" she asked, satisfaction seeping into her voice.

"Nope. It took off right on time. In fact, it should be landing in Laramie in another five minutes."

"Then what are you doing here?"

"Like I said, I wouldn't think of leaving you behind."

Casey felt her anger flare and she spun around to face him again. "You did leave me behind! You got on that plane without me. You deserted me."

"I never intended to desert you, Carmichael. Can I have the rest of that burger?" he asked, grabbing it before she had a chance to refuse. He continued his explanation as he wolfed it down. "I just thought the only way to get you on that plane was if I got on without you. I thought for sure you'd be mad enough to follow me. And when you didn't, I got off."

"Don't you dare try to convince me your motives were honorable, you snake! You had every intention of leaving me here."

Matt smiled ruefully, scooping up the last of her fries. "I didn't then, but I'm beginning to think it's not such a bad idea. I've been looking all over this damn airport for you. Why didn't you stick around and watch the plane leave? I wasn't counting on you running off like that."

"And torture myself further? I had important business to take care of. Like hiring a snitch to follow *you* at the Laramie airport."

Matt stood up and took her elbow. "Clever girl," he said with what sounded like admiration. "You might just make an investigative reporter yet. You're resourceful, you're determined and you're certainly stubborn enough. Come on, let's go."

Casey yanked her arm away, annoyed that she felt pleased at his offhand compliment. "I'm not going anywhere with you. As of now, our partnership is officially dissolved."

"All right, if you want to sit here in this airport all night, that's up to you. But I'm leaving for Laramie now, and I thought you might want to come with me."

"I'm not getting on a plane with you."

"And I'm not getting on a plane with you, either, Ms. Carmichael," he said in humorous condescension. "We're going to rent a car and drive."

Casey felt new hope begin to bloom but it faded quickly. "Now? But it's snowing like crazy out there. We can't drive in this kind of weather."

"I've driven in a lot worse than this. In good weather, Laramie is less than three hours away. In this weather, I figure we can get there in four or five. If we rent a four by four, maybe less."

Casey considered her options, but after a few seconds of thought she realized, once again, he had left her with no options. She would have to go with him or risk losing the story. But the games between them would have to stop. It was time to come to a firm agreement about their working relationship.

"I will go with you on one condition," she explained, standing to face him. "No more games. No lies, no tricks. I promise I will be completely straightforward with you, if you will promise the same to me."

Matt arched his eyebrow and gave her a dubious look. "If you'll remember, Carmichael, you're the one who's been doing the lion's share of the lying. *You* agreed to a partnership that night in your apartment, then reneged on the deal."

"The past is past," she countered. "Do we have a deal?"

He nodded his head. "We have a deal, Carmichael," he answered in a sexy voice.

"Partners?"

"Partners."

"*Equal* partners," she amended.

Casey held out her hand and Matt took it, lacing his fingers through hers, and brought her hand to his lips. With a seductive smile, he ran his warm lips along her knuckles. She shivered, wanting to snatch her hand from his, yet wanting him to go on caressing her fingers with his mouth. Pulling her closer, he wrapped his arm around her back and pinned her against his chest. His sapphire blue eyes stared intently into hers. Desire flickered in their depths, darkening the color to a midnight blue.

He lowered his head, his lips nearly touching hers. "No more games, Casey."

He waited for her reaction, but she was mesmerized by his gaze, weak with her own tightly controlled passion and determined not to let her warring emotions show in her expression.

He paused for a moment, studying her face as if he was carefully considering his actions. Then, as quickly as it had appeared, the spark of desire that glittered in his eyes was gone. He stepped away from her, took her hand and shook it firmly. "Right," he said, his voice soft and distracted. "Equal partners."

TRUE TO HIS WORD, they reached Laramie exactly four hours later. Keeping the Blazer on the road was an ongoing battle, but Matt was used to traveling under harsh conditions. The challenge of getting to a story was sometimes more fun than the story itself. He had battled wind and ice on Mount McKinley, rain and insects on a trip down the Amazon, and sand in the north of Africa. A little snow was only a minor annoyance.

Matt glanced over at Casey to find her still sitting with her eyes squeezed tightly shut. She had been that way for most of the trip, trying to quell the hypnotic effects of staring into the oncoming snow. When Matt pulled into the parking lot of a brightly lit discount store, she finally opened her eyes and let her tense body relax.

"I feel like I've just spent four hours on the roller coaster at Magic Mountain. What are we stopping here for?" she asked. "I saw some restaurants down the road. Let's get something to eat. I'm hungry."

"I need to pick up a few things. You wait right here and I'll be out in a minute."

"Wait, I'll come in with you," Casey cried, scrambling to find her damp shoes. Matt looked down at the shapeless little slippers she had worn. One trip from the truck to a gas-station bathroom was all it had taken to ruin her footwear. And her flimsy jacket didn't do much against the biting wind that howled unceasingly out of the Rockies. She had come totally unprepared for the weather.

Matt snatched one of her shoes and shoved it into his pocket. "I said wait here. I'll be back in a few minutes." With that, he slammed the door of the truck.

Her muffled shout from inside the truck made him smile. "I thought we were supposed to be equal partners," she yelled.

Partners. They had made a pact at the airport. No more lies and deception. He had agreed to the pact with no intention of keeping his word. He had what he needed from Casey and he had been rid of her when he boarded the plane. But something drew him back. The hell of it was he didn't know why.

He grabbed a cart and he made his way through the deserted aisles to the women's clothing department. He had been formulating plans during the long ride to Laramie. Depositing Casey at the nearest motel had been Plan A. But he doubted that she would let him out of her sight. He was stuck with her at least until they got the story. Buying her warm clothes was part of Plan B. After choosing a selection of suitable winter wear, Matt headed for the checkout counter.

Why *had* he gone back? Why hadn't he stayed on the plane to Laramie? Maybe he felt sorry for her. She had been a pretty pitiful sight, standing in the snow, shouting at him, trying desperately to overcome her fears.

*Be honest, Garrison. It wasn't pity that brought you back.*

So if it wasn't pity, what was it? Admiration? He did admire her tenacity. Even after he'd walked out on her, she'd been determined to get the story. Concern? Casey Carmichael could certainly take care of herself. Still, he did feel a nagging sense of responsibility for her. Honor? Since when had he acted honorably toward any woman?

Maybe it was just lust, pure and simple. He wanted Casey Carmichael. He had wanted her from the start. She was a challenge. For every indication she gave of not wanting him, his need for her increased. He wanted to lose himself in her just once, turn her into just another conquest to break the strange magnetic hold she had over him. As the past had proven, once the challenge was met, he could move on and leave her behind.

At the last moment, he made a detour through health aids and tossed a small box into his cart. Plan C, he thought to himself with a smile. If it was lust, just maybe he'd get lucky tonight.

The truck was covered with a dusting of snow when he returned. He pulled the door open and tossed the bags in Casey's direction as he slid into the driver's seat. "Here, don't say I never gave you anything."

Casey regarded him angrily from the far side of the seat. "What's this?" she asked.

"Open it and find out." Matt started the truck and pulled out of the parking lot, his eyes fixed on a motel sign down the road.

Casey peered into the largest of the bags and pulled out the jacket he had purchased. He watched her examine the garment, a look of genuine distaste wrinkling her nose.

"This has got to be the most . . . unusual jacket I have ever seen," she said as she carefully examined the drab olive green shell and the blaze orange lining. She seemed fascinated by the snorkel hood and the multitude of pockets and buttons, both inside and out. "I think you should have taken me with you. I could have found a much nicer jacket for you."

"It's not for me," Matt explained. "It's for you."

"I'm not going to wear this," Casey said, pushing the garment back at him. "It's the ugliest jacket I've ever seen."

"It may be ugly, but it's the warmest I could find. It's down-filled and it's long, so it will keep your darling little derriere warm."

"Thanks, but no thanks." She tossed the jacket into the back of the truck and slouched down in her seat, putting an end to their brief conversation.

"Listen, Carmichael. I don't think you understand what's ahead of us. Once we find Emily, I don't think she's going to welcome us with open arms. We're going to have to keep a low profile and that might mean watching her from outside rather than inside. In case you haven't noticed, it's cold outside and you are not dressed for the occasion. So put the damn jacket on."

Her jaw was set and she raised her chin indignantly. "Don't you try to bully me, Garrison. It won't work."

Matt felt his temper flare. Why did she have to fight him every step of the way? Couldn't she trust him just a little bit? After all, he had gone back for her at the airport. And he had stopped to buy her warm clothing. He turned the truck into the motel parking lot and skidded to a stop. "Either you put the jacket on, or I'm dumping you right here."

"Try it," she challenged.

He reached across her lap and pushed open the passenger-side door. "Don't tempt me."

Casey opened her mouth to protest, then gave him a sugary smile. "All right," she said. "Thank you for the lovely jacket, Garrison."

Matt pulled the door shut, then grabbed the bags and pulled out the clothing he had purchased—two heavy wool sweaters, a turtleneck, a set of long underwear, two pairs of wool socks, a pair of jeans and finally, a pair of industrial-strength boots. "You might as well put these on, too."

She snatched the boots up and examined them carefully. They had a soft felt lining and leather laces up the front. He steeled himself for another round of protest. Although the boots were about as attractive as the jacket, they promised to protect her feet from the nagging cold.

To his surprise, she tugged them on over her thin socks, then sighed. "They're ugly, but they'll do the trick."

"Hold on a second," Matt said. "Pull those boots off and put these on." He handed her the long underwear, a pair of socks and the jeans.

"I'll try those on after we find a motel," Casey answered, still luxuriating in the warmth of her new boots.

Matt put the truck into gear and headed back out to the road. "We're not stopping for the night. At least not yet. First I want to check out this ranch where Emily's staying. It's supposed to be only a half hour from the city, so I figured we'd drive out there and scout around a little."

"Now?" Casey asked, blinking in disbelief. "But it's dark out. And it's still snowing. We won't be able to see anything. Let's just get a couple of rooms and go out there in the morning. It'll be light then."

"Yes it will, Sherlock. And when it's light, we'll have a much better chance of being seen. I want to know what we're up against. The best way to find out is to nose around under the cover of darkness."

"You don't think anybody else is onto this lead, do you?"

"Not unless you told someone where we were going. You didn't, did you?" he asked, a hint of accusation in his voice.

"Of course not."

"Griswold told me he had an inside tip on the wedding and I'm sure he hasn't told anyone outside of the staff at *The Inquisitor*. A couple of the staff writers have been parked outside Emily's house for the last few days and one guy flew to New York to tail her fiancé, but you and I are the only people who know about her trip to Laramie. My guess is, if the wedding *is* planned for the ranch, we've got a lock on this story. And a cool twenty-five thousand dollars. Now put those things on."

"Here?" she asked. "Can't we stop at a gas station? I can change in the bathroom."

"We don't have time. It's already after ten and it's going to take us a while to get out there." He looked over at her with a devilish smile. "Don't worry, I won't look."

As she struggled out of her pleated khaki trousers, he made a valiant attempt to keep his eyes fixed on the road, but the thought of Casey Carmichael removing her clothes in his presence was too much to resist. He turned to watch her brace her bare feet against the dashboard as she concentrated on tugging the close-fitting long underwear over her slender legs. An image of those incredible legs wrapped around his waist flickered through his mind. His gaze drifted along her thigh then stopped suddenly at her words.

"I thought you weren't going to look."

Matt blinked and looked at her, grinning, then turned his attention back to the road. "I lied."

"You know," she continued as she pulled on the blue jeans, "you couldn't have chosen less attractive clothing if you'd tried."

"It fits, doesn't it?"

He watched her pull the turtleneck over her head, noting how she avoided removing her blouse first. One of the wool sweaters followed. To his surprise, everything did fit. She pulled the jacket on and snuggled into its down-filled depths. For the first time since they'd left the airport in Denver, she looked happy, content, approachable.

"Besides," Matt said, "a flour sack would look good on you."

"Was that a compliment, Garrison?" she asked, her voice leery.

Matt shook his head, quickly denying the truth. "Nope, just an observation. I don't want my partner dying of hypothermia on me, do I?"

Although, considering Casey Carmichael's icy opinion of him, hypothermia might be an improvement.

THEY HAD BEEN DRIVING for nearly fifty minutes when Matt stopped the truck in the middle of a desolate, snow-drifted road. He pulled a piece of paper from his jacket pocket then flipped on the overhead light, squinting in its glare.

"What's wrong?" Casey asked, uncomfortable with the irritated look in his eyes.

"Nothing." He threw the truck back into gear and revved the engine, sending the truck fishtailing down the road.

"You agreed that we would be equal partners," Casey insisted. "I have a right to know what's going on. Now, what's wrong?"

"I said nothing is wrong," he answered angrily.

Casey watched his jaw clench and his eyes search the road ahead. "We're lost, aren't we."

"No. I'm just not sure exactly where we are at the moment," he explained, as if talking to a small child. "But as soon as we come to a crossroad, we won't be lost anymore. Then I'll know where we are."

Casey bristled at his stubborn attitude, but her anger was gradually replaced by a feeling of panic. "I told you we should have stayed in Laramie. The snow's been getting worse since we left the city. This road doesn't look like it's been plowed, it's pitch-black out, we can't see ten feet in front of the truck, and you don't know where we are. I'd say we're not just lost, we're in big trouble. I think we should turn this truck around and go back to Laramie."

"We are not lost. Not yet," he insisted, though his voice betrayed his real thoughts. "The ranch is along this road. It's probably just around the next curve."

Casey's throat tightened. "Garrison, turn the truck around. In this snow we could drive off the side of a cliff and not know it until we hit the ground." She reached for his arm, but he pulled away from her, his hand yanking the wheel sharply to the left.

The Blazer started a slow skid beneath them. Matt tried frantically to bring the spinning vehicle back under control but the four by four continued its uncontrolled slide toward the edge of the road. As the headlights illuminated the trees, Casey closed her eyes and waited for the impact. She felt the truck sink first in front, then in the rear, before coming to a final stop with a soft *whump*. She slowly opened her eyes, surprised at their soft landing. The truck was tipped at a slight angle, one side caught in the ditch and the other side parallel to the road.

"Are you all right?" Matt asked.

"Yes. Are you?" Casey answered, her voice strained.

He was silent for several moments, then let out a pent-up breath. "Yeah," he said, lowering his forehead to rest on the steering wheel. "I'm sorry, Casey. You were right. As soon as we get this truck out of the ditch, we'll go back to Laramie. It was stupid of me to take a chance with your safety."

Casey reached out to run her hand along the sleeve of his leather jacket. "It's all right. You didn't force me to come with you. I want this story as much as you do and I'm willing to take a few chances to get it."

"I'm used to being responsible for one person, and that's me," he said, jerking his head up and slamming his hand against the steering wheel. "I can afford to take a few risks if I'm the only one who can get hurt. I'm not used to worrying about another person, that's all."

"Really, Garrison," Casey said, tightening her grip on his arm, "it's all right. Let's get this truck out of the ditch and get back to Laramie. We can try this road again in the morning."

Matt nodded and returned her smile apologetically. But his smile turned to a frown the moment he put the truck in reverse and touched the gas pedal. The sound of spinning wheels nearly drowned out the sound of Matt cursing. He put the truck in forward with the same result. The panicky feeling crept through Casey's body again and she looked over at Matt, silently urging him on.

With a shout of disgust, he rammed the truck into park and shut off the engine. "So much for good intentions," he said with a sardonic laugh. "We are stuck and stuck good. It feels like we're wedged in pretty tight. I could try to dig us out, but I'm afraid that wouldn't do much good. And I don't have a shovel, either," he added.

"We could walk down the road and see if there's a house nearby. We could call a tow truck from there," Casey offered.

"I think it would be best if we stay put. Like you said, the snow is getting worse. It's awfully easy to lose your way in weather like this. We're safer if we stay with the truck. When the plow comes through they'll call someone to pull us out."

"Do we have enough gas to keep the truck running all night?"

"Yes, but we're not going to."

"But it's so cold. We'll freeze if we stay out here."

"If we leave the engine on, the snow might drift over the exhaust pipe and we might die of carbon monoxide poisoning. Besides we don't need the heat, it's not much below freezing outside. We're out of the wind. Our body heat will warm up the truck. You can put on a few more layers of clothing. And I've got my down sleeping bag. We're all set."

"Sure, we're all set," she snapped. "Two weeks from now, when the plow finally comes to this godforsaken excuse for a road, they'll find us frozen rock solid. I still think we should try to find help."

"Casey, don't worry, help will find us. Trust me on this."

"Trust you. Now there's a novel thought," she muttered.

Matt flipped on the overhead light, climbed into the back seat, and leaned over into the cargo area to rummage through his backpack. Casey grudgingly followed his lead and pulled the second sweater he had bought for her over the first. The task was made more difficult by the precarious angle of the truck, and she had to brace her feet against the driver's seat to maintain her balance. The second pair of wool socks then followed the extra sweater. For good measure, she tugged her baggy khaki pants on over the jeans and by the time she was finished wrestling her jacket back on she had actually worked up a sweat. Thank goodness Matt had thought to buy her more sensible clothes. She never would have survived the cold in the clothes she had brought with her.

She turned to find Matt stretched out on the back seat, leaning against the low side of the truck, his feet resting on the opposite armrest. A puffy red sleeping bag was spread over his legs. His jacket was unzipped and she could see that he still wore a thin cotton T-shirt underneath. "Aren't you going to put more clothes on?" she asked, her gaze fixed on the shirt pulled tight over the muscles of his chest.

He smiled disarmingly. "I'll be plenty warm once you join me back here." He lifted the sleeping bag up in an invitation.

"N-no thanks, I'll just sleep up here."

"Don't be silly, Casey. We can share our warmth. It's nice and warm under here. Come on, I promise I won't try anything. You can trust me."

"Ha, there's that word again. Trusting you is what got us into this mess."

Casey flipped off the light and climbed into the back seat opposite him on the high side of the truck. But try as she might, she kept sliding down toward him. The only possible place to brace her feet was between his legs. Though the thought of causing Matt Garrison a little pain appealed to her, the thought of coming into intimate contact with his body would most likely cause her a great deal more discomfort.

Frustrated with her feeble attempts to perch on the seat, Matt dragged her toward him, settled her back against his chest and slid her narrow hips between his thighs. He pulled the sleeping bag up over them both then wrapped his arms around her.

Her pulse began to pound as her nerve endings became aware of the feel of him, his hard muscular thighs shifting against her legs, his wide chest pressed against her back, his arms wrapped around her midsection, nearly touching the underside of her breasts. Even through the multiple layers of clothing, she could feel his heat and she longed to press herself more closely to him, to turn in his arms and bury her face in the curve of his neck. He would kiss her then, soft and long and deep, as he had in the hotel room, only this time he would linger over her mouth.

He seemed unaffected by their close contact, his arms wrapped casually around her waist. Though she knew she should be happy that he was not making any seductive moves, secretly she was disappointed. Just what would it feel like to be seduced by Matt Garrison? Better yet, what would it feel like to have the power to seduce him? How would it feel to turn the tables on him, to make him lose control?

She turned the delicious thought around her mind, wondering if she would ever have the courage to make a sexual advance toward a man, especially a man as handsome as Garrison.

Theodora could do it. Theodora wouldn't have any qualms about using sex as a weapon. Theodora would . . .

*But I'm Theodora*, Casey thought in surprise. *She's me. Whatever she can do, I can. Maybe not as well, but well enough to get by.*

Matt tightened his hold on her. "Comfortable?" he asked, his voice warm and soothing.

She stiffened slightly at his words, then willed her body to relax. "Yes," she replied, closing her eyes and drawing a deep breath. "This really isn't too bad. I think I just might survive."

"Of course you'll survive. This is an adventure. Not only will you survive, you'll tell all your friends about the night you were stranded in the middle of nowhere in a raging blizzard in a rented truck . . . with me."

"You're enjoying this, aren't you?"

"Everyone likes adventure. Living on the edge gets my blood pumping. I like never knowing what's around the next corner. Haven't you ever had an adventure?"

His warm breath teased her ear and she could see it puffing in the cold. "Once maybe, when I was nine years old. I guess you could call it an adventure, though it didn't seem so at the time. In fact, it was downright scary as I recall."

"Tell me about it," he said, resting his chin on her shoulder.

"Louise was working in California then. I was sent out to visit her for the summer and she got it into her head that she needed to take me to Las Vegas. I would have been satisfied with a day at Disneyland, but she said Vegas was much more exciting. So we hopped into a beat-up old station wagon and drove from Bakersfield to Las Vegas. We didn't have much money, so when we got there Louise decided to head right for the casinos and try to win a little. She sat me down on a couch in the lobby of the hotel and went into the casino and didn't come back for three hours. I was so terrified I didn't move from the spot, thinking that if I did, she'd leave without me. When she came back she had a wad of money in her hand. We rented a fancy room with a marble bathtub and red velvet drapes. I remember her throwing the money up in the air over the bed and then rolling around in it."

"That sounds like an adventure to me."

"Wait," Casey warned. "It gets better. Or worse, depending on the way you look at it. The next day we went to the beauty shop and she had the hairdresser bleach my hair blond and paint my fingernails fire-engine red. She said we looked just like sisters and that I was so much prettier as a blonde. Then she sat me down in the lobby and went into the casino again. This time when she came out she didn't have any money. That night we slept in the car. We slept in the car for three more nights before we went home. I was so upset that when we got back to Bakersfield, I made her send me home early.

"When I went back to school a few weeks later with bleached blond hair all the girls thought it was so cool. They all said they wished they had a mother like mine. I started to think it was pretty cool, too, until my hair started to grow out. My grandmother took me to the local beauty shop to dye my hair red again, but it turned an attractive shade of green. And that brought an abrupt end to my instant celebrity and my dreams of becoming the next Sandra Dee."

"I think this adventure pales in comparison to that one. Your mother sounds like a real character."

Casey laughed dryly. "Yes, my mother was a real character. Most times I felt like the grown-up around her. There were times when I just wanted her to take care of me, instead of the other way around. I wanted to lock her up in a house and force her to be a mother, just like the kind the other kids had. I wanted a regular family."

"Yeah, that's pretty much what I wanted when I was a kid, too."

"And now? What do you want now?"

"Freedom. No ties, no responsibilities, nothing to hold me back. And enough money to keep me going for a few years."

"And that's it? Don't you want more?"

"What more is there? I have everything I could possibly want."

"What about a place to come home to?" *And a person to come home to*, her mind added.

"A house is just another unneeded possession. I can carry everything I own in two hands. It makes life very simple."

She had known they were different from the start, but now a vast gulf had sprung up between them. All the symptoms of wanderlust that she had seen in her mother were alive and well in Matt Garrison. Her heart twisted at the realization that, no matter how much she wanted him to fall in love with her, he never would.

Yet, even knowing that, she knew it would be hard to keep herself from falling in love with him. If she wasn't already hopelessly in love. She would just have to prepare for the pain that lay ahead. Loving Matt Garrison was a doomed cause.

"I'm tired," she said, her voice cold and remote. "We'd better get some sleep." She closed her eyes, but his handsome face refused to disappear. In her mind he was there, above her, looking down into her eyes with a gaze that promised unbridled passion and uncontrolled pleasure.

She felt Matt's warm lips brush against her cheek. "Good night, Casey."

"Good night, Garrison," she replied.

Casey lay with her back against his chest and stared straight ahead into the darkness, her body stiff and her mind numb. Why was she cursed with the ability to love all the wrong people? And why were the people she loved the most cursed with the inability to love her in return?

# 5

*His fingers were warm and hard as they slipped
around my wrist. Slowly, he took the gun from my
hand and let it drop to the floor. Then he pulled me
into his arms and covered my mouth with his,
kissing me until my mind reeled and my senses
screamed. He buried his face in the curve of my
neck, whispering explicit promises of the passion
to come. My mind had ceased to function, my
body was being driven by pleasure alone, and I
went weak in his embrace. His breath was hot
against my ear. "I want you, Theo" he moaned.
"Then take me," I murmured, my voice clouded
by desire. "Take me now." Take me, take me, take
me . . .*

AS SHE DRIFTED in the peaceful languor between sleep
and wakefulness Casey felt warm hands sliding along
her stomach and grazing her rib cage, skin upon skin.
Still anchored in the world of dreams she twisted
slightly to allow the questing fingers to move higher,
and a tiny thrill shot through her as the hands skimmed
over her breasts, causing her nipples to tingle beneath
the filmy fabric of her bra.

She opened her eyes slowly and was confused by her
surroundings. Was this part of the dream, this bright

white light that surrounded her? Where was she? What were these incredible sensations that coursed through her body? She wanted to remain within the hazy confines of her dream, but her mind began to pull her to the surface, into the realm of consciousness.

She became aware of slow, even breathing, movement against her back and beneath her. She felt undeniable pleasure, unfamiliar yet instinctively understood. She moved again to try to get closer to the source of her pleasure: warm, hard fingers and smooth palms. As she twisted from her back to her side, her eye caught the bright orange and drab green of her jacket lying in a crumpled heap.

The color brought her fully awake. As she turned, she heard Matt moan slightly. She felt the evidence of his arousal, rigid and hot beneath her hip, yet restrained by several layers of clothing. His hands still caressed her, moving to rotate his palms over the hardened buds of her nipples. She wanted to pull away, to speak to him and wake him, but the feelings he was bringing forth in her were too overwhelming to resist.

She turned more fully to him and his hands moved down her back to grasp her buttocks and pull her between his thighs, more tightly against his straining hardness. She risked a glance up at him and saw that his eyes were closed, as if he, too, was caught between dark and dawn, unaware of his actions and the pleasure they were giving her.

All her instincts rebelled at the thought of waking him, but she wanted more than just her own pleasure in a solitary void. She could not fight this attraction any longer.

*Open your eyes, Matt. Look at me.*

She wanted him to know that he touched her, to see her arousal reflected in his eyes. Lord, she wanted him, more than she had ever wanted anything in her life. But she needed him to be awake and aware. And most of all, she needed him to steer a straight and gentle course through her bewildered senses to wherever this undeniable passion might lead.

She spread her fingers gently over the taut fabric of his T-shirt and pushed his jacket aside. Taking a deep breath, Casey felt her resolve strengthen. She slid along his body to touch her mouth to his, shyly running the tip of her tongue along his lower lip. His mouth was firm and sensual, just as she remembered it.

His eyes opened languidly and she could see confusion, need and then suspicion in their steamy blue depths. He watched her, unmoving, caught between desire and denial.

It was now or never, she thought to herself. She would have to be the one to initiate the next step, for she was certain that if she didn't make a move, the spell would be broken and his rational mind would put a stop to what his impulses began.

She should have been nervous, but her inhibitions had fled long ago and she was driven by a need to know him in a purely physical way. Their magical surroundings and the haziness of sleep had erased the lack of confidence and the underlying embarrassment she had experienced in her past intimacies with men.

Casey moved to kiss him again, but at the last moment, he pulled his head back and avoided her touch, watching her in uncertainty. Casey felt her heart twist in her chest. He was going to call an end to it. She closed her eyes in humiliation. He didn't want her. She had been wrong. Naively and stupidly wrong.

Then suddenly, she felt him draw her closer. Casey opened her eyes to see his mouth come up to meet hers. Slowly, he began a gentle assault with his lips and tongue. A shiver of relief swept through her and she surrendered herself to his kiss, opening her mouth to his and meeting every thrust of his tongue.

Without breaking contact, he brought her up to straddle his hips. His hands spanned her narrow waist and pushed her firmly down to meet his hard arousal, touching but not touching her in the most intimate of places. A moan escaped her throat as she pulled her lips from his, arched sinuously and threw her head back. She came back to him and slid her delicate fingers beneath his shirt, along the narrow strip of hair that began at the waistband of his jeans and across the washboard ripples of his stomach to rake over the smooth contours of his broad chest. Her nails scraped his pebble-hard nipples and she heard him draw a sharp breath.

The only sounds that broke the crystalline silence were the sounds of their breathing and the rustle of their movements. Casey realized that they hadn't spoken a word to each other. Their communication was done purely by touch and an intense stare that caught every nuance of desire in the other's expression.

The connection was broken momentarily as Matt pulled her sweater up and over her head. Layer by layer, he peeled her clothes from the top half of her body until she wore only the sheer covering of her bra. The cold felt good on her heated skin. He reached out and cupped her breasts in his palms, and teased the hardened tips through the slippery fabric with the pads of his thumbs.

A tremulous smile tugged at Casey's lips as he looked up at her, his dark hair rumpled and his eyes clouded with passion. Slowly, she ran a fingernail along the line of his jaw, scraping the surface of his beard-roughened face, and moved to trace the thin line of the scar on his chin.

He pulled her to him and kissed her again, this time harder and more impatiently, and ran his fingers through her tangled hair, moving her mouth against his until he was satisfied with the depth of their kiss. Casey felt the blood rushing though her veins, the pounding pressure of her pulse echoing in her head.

Then he pulled away. He was gone. Opening her eyes, she looked down at him and watched his brow furrow in confusion. "What is it?" she asked, her voice husky with unfulfilled passion. A rush of self-doubt numbed her quivering nerves as she saw the distracted look on his face. "A-am I doing something wrong?"

"There's someone out there."

Casey froze and listened carefully. She jumped as if she had been doused with ice water when she heard the sounds. Someone or something was tapping on the window of the truck. In a flurry of movement, she pushed herself off Matt and scrambled for the far side of the seat. She grabbed her sweater and yanked it over her head, then began a frenzied search for her discarded glasses.

The tapping continued on the window of the passenger side. "Hello, is anyone in there?" a muffled female voice called. The windows were covered by a thick layer of white that diffused the morning light, but as Casey watched, some of the snow fell away from the window and revealed a small hand encased in a red mitten.

Matt pulled his T-shirt down and calmly zipped his jacket, avoiding her wide-eyed gaze. She thought she noticed a slight flush of embarrassment stain his cheeks before he turned and climbed into the front seat to open the door.

As he pushed open the door, a cloud of snowflakes blew into the truck and clung like sparking shards of diamonds to his hair and lashes. He shook his head in annoyance, then smiled as he spoke.

"Hi, there. Boy, are we happy to see you." Casey wondered if he really meant what he said or if the tiny catch of sarcasm in his voice revealed his true feelings. When he jumped out of the truck and slammed the door behind him, she hurried to put on her jacket, anxious to meet their rescuer.

By the time she struggled out the door, Matt was examining the front wheels of the truck, soberly assessing the situation with a slight figure bundled in layers of clothing. The woman's features were completely hidden by a scarf that was tightly wrapped around her nose and mouth, a ski cap that covered her hair, and a pair of sunglasses that protected her eyes from the blowing snow and bright white light.

As Casey watched them, she felt a nudge on her back and wondered if the woman had brought a companion. She turned to offer a friendly greeting, but came nose to nose with an enormous animal. She let out a shriek that echoed through the woods.

Casey stumbled through the heavy drifts toward Matt trying to put some distance between her and the beast, but tripped and tumbled headfirst into a snow-drift. She floundered as she tried to stand up, then felt familiar strong hands encircle her waist and pull her from the snow. Matt was grinning as he removed her snow-caked glasses, roughly brushed the snow from her face and clothing and pushed her unbound hair out of her eyes. Another nudge against her shoulder sent her scampering to safety behind him.

Clinging tightly to Matt's biceps, she peered over his shoulder into the liquid brown eyes of a large horse. The animal seemed to be smiling at her as if he wanted to make friends.

"Jesse, stop that," the woman cried. "Leave the nice lady alone." She rushed up to the horse and grabbed the loose reins, then patted the animal and rubbed her cheek against its nose. She turned to Casey and Matt. "Don't mind Jesse. He's just looking for food. He can be such a moocher." She held out her mittened hand to Casey. "I'm Ellen Hansen."

Matt put his arm around Casey's shoulders and dug his fingers into her upper arm. With a questioning look Casey twisted away from him in irritation, then offered her hand. "Hi, Ellen, I'm Casey—"

"Garrison," Matt interrupted. "Ellen, this is my wife, Casey." Casey looked over at Matt in disbelief. What was he talking about? His wife? What kind of game was he playing now? But there it was again, the same expression she had seen in Finkleman's hotel room. Trust me, his gaze pleaded. Trust me.

Casey covered her confusion with a smile and shook Ellen's hand firmly, keeping one watchful eye on the black beast Jesse.

"I was telling your husband that I rode out here to see if the roads had been plowed and found your truck in the ditch, not twenty yards from the end of my driveway. I'm sorry you had to spend the night in the cold. Had you gotten a few feet farther, you may have been able to see the lights from the house through the trees."

"It wasn't so bad," Matt answered, looking over at Casey for a moment. "We kept each other warm. Didn't we, darlin'?" He slipped his arm around her shoulders again and pulled her to his side.

"Well, why don't you come up to the house with me and warm up. We can call a tow truck to pull you out, though it may take a while. They won't come out on this road until the snow's been plowed and it usually doesn't get plowed until it stops snowing." Ellen looked at the clouds building on the horizon. "It's let up for a while, but it's supposed to start again and keep snowing all day today and into the night."

"That's mighty nice of you to offer your hospitality, ma'am, but we wouldn't want to impose. We can wait out here for the plow."

Casey glanced up at Matt in shock. What did he think he was doing? Was he crazy? She wasn't about to spend the next minute, much less the next day and possibly another night, sitting it out in the cold when someone was offering a warm house.

"Don't be silly," Ellen answered. "It's no imposition. In fact, I'd enjoy the company. I'm alone up there except for the ranch foreman and his crew. And they don't offer much in the line of stimulating conversation. Get your things and we'll throw them on Jesse's back."

Casey smiled in relief and jumped in before Matt lodged any further protests. "Thank you, Ellen. I have to admit, a warm house sounds awfully good right now." And indoor plumbing, Casey added in her mind, sounded even better.

The hike up the long drive was slow and exhausting. Three-foot-deep drifts hindered their progress and they didn't speak, preferring to concentrate their efforts and energies on the struggle to wallow through the snow. Casey glanced at Matt every few seconds, wondering if he was also mentally replaying the early morning events as she was.

When Casey saw the sprawling ranch house at the top of a small rise, she quickened her pace, anxious to get out of the biting wind and into a warm house. The smell of burning wood reached her nose and she looked up to see wisps of smoke blown about by the wind from the top of a fieldstone chimney.

She was amazed at the rustic beauty of the house. Made of rough-hewn logs with a cedar-shingle roof, it was one with the woods around it. A wide porch spanned the length of the house and large windows overlooked the drive. Something about the house reminded her of her grandparents' home. Maybe it was the setting or the building materials. Though the two were widely disparate in size, a feeling of recognition warmed her heart.

"What a lovely home," Casey said.

"Thank you," Ellen answered. "Though I must admit, it doesn't belong to me. I'm just visiting for a few days. It actually belongs to a good friend of mine. Big as it is, it does have a nice homey feel to it."

Ellen tied Jesse's reins to the front porch rail, and Matt lifted Casey's bags off the horn of the saddle, then they followed Ellen into the foyer of the house. Its rustic exterior gave no hint of the elegance inside. Though the decor was decidedly Western in flavor, lovely antiques were visible through the open archways of the dining room and living area.

"Why don't you leave your things here," Ellen suggested as she began to pull off her hat and scarf. She struggled a moment with her boots and turned away to rest her hand on the arm of an antique deacon's bench. Slipping out of her jacket she turned back to them, a bright smile on her face.

Casey felt her breath leave her body. Emily Harrington! She was staring into the face of Emily Harrington! Though she wore no makeup and her hair was pulled away from her face in a casual ponytail, Casey would have recognized her smile anywhere.

"Ellen, why don't you show me where the phone is and I'll try calling a tow truck," Matt said smoothly, his voice betraying no surprise at the woman's appearance. "Though we may have to wait in line. This weather's probably caused all sorts of accidents."

Casey turned to look at Matt, trying to catch his eye. Didn't he recognize her? Ellen's real identity had to be obvious, even to the most obtuse observer.

Emily pointed to a phone on an old rolltop desk in the living room. "There's a phone book in the top drawer. Why don't you call while I make us a pot of coffee? Casey, the powder room is right down this hall." Emily smiled at her in understanding, before turning to make her way to the back of the house and the kitchen.

As soon as she was out of view, Matt grabbed Casey by the hand and pulled her into the living room. His touch caused a quiver of excitement to rush up her arm and through her body. "I can't believe our luck!" he whispered in amazement.

Casey lowered her own voice. "I was wondering if you recognized her. Why were you acting so thick? And what was that thing about waiting in the truck for the snowplow? We would never have known it was her!"

"I knew it was her the moment she introduced herself. Emily Harrington is just her professional name. Her real name is Ellen Hansen. Ellen Hansen from Minnetonka, Minnesota."

"That still doesn't explain why you offered to wait in the truck."

"Come on, Sherlock, figure it out. If she thinks we know who she is, she'll show us the door in three seconds flat. But, if she believes we don't recognize her, maybe she'll let us visit awhile."

He was absolutely right. Matt Garrison might be a scoundrel, but she was glad he possessed the ability to think on his feet. They were inside the house with Emily Harrington. They had the opportunity to gain her trust. And even if the wedding didn't take place at the ranch, they'd have a terrific story to turn in to *The Inquisitor.* In the process, they might even be able to pick up some clues as to the time and location of the wedding.

"So what do we do next?" Casey asked.

"Just act like you don't recognize her. We're supposed to be married, so pretend to be the dutiful little wife and let me do most of the talking."

Casey felt her temper begin to rise. Equal partners? How quickly he forgot. "Why did you have to tell her we were married?"

"It seemed like the logical thing to do. Being a member of the married race invites fewer questions, believe me." The sound of footsteps echoed on the slate-tiled floor of the hallway.

"She's coming back," Casey warned.

Matt looked up, then quickly pulled the phone book from the drawer of the desk and threw it onto the spotless surface. He picked up the phone and held it to his ear. "Whatever you do, Carmichael, don't call her Emily. From now on she is Ellen. Ellen, not Emily."

Ellen appeared at the entrance to the living room, just as Matt put the phone back in its cradle. "Were you able to find a tow truck?"

Matt shook his head. "Nope. I called three places and they said it would be at least a day before they could come out this far."

Ellen looked at them both sympathetically. "That's too bad. Are you supposed to be somewhere soon?"

"Not really. We just came up here to take some photos."

Ellen's expression turned cold. "You're a photographer?"

"A nature photographer. I'd hoped to take some shots of the elk and mule deer in their winter habitat. But we got lost driving on these back roads with the snow and all. We'll need to find a cheap place to spend the night. A photographer's income doesn't leave much money for fancy hotels."

Casey could see the relief in Ellen's eyes. "I suppose it doesn't." She paused for a moment, studying them both, then her expression brightened. "Why don't you stay here tonight? There's plenty of room and I'd enjoy the company. My fiancé was supposed to fly in this afternoon, but with the blizzard he may be delayed. It would be nice not to have to spend another night alone in this house. And tomorrow morning, if the tow truck doesn't come, I'll see if the ranch hands can get your truck out of the ditch."

Matt looked at her as if considering her offer, then turned to Casey. His eyes glittered with suppressed excitement. Her fiancé? Casey was ready to wager her meager life savings on the fact that there would be a wedding in this house within the week. She looked up at him, trying to hide the anticipation in her eyes, then shrugged her shoulders, not willing to say anything to put the offer in jeopardy.

Matt turned his most charming smile on Ellen. "Thank you. That's a real nice offer, Ellen. We'd be happy to stay."

THEY WERE GIVEN a room at the back of the house, with a bank of multipaned windows overlooking a stunning winter vista of tall ponderosa pines and a thin stand of leafless aspens. Visible through the trees was a frozen lake, its ice gleaming and windswept, surrounded by a wide meadow carpeted with dunes of white.

The large four-poster that dominated the room was covered with a fluffy white down comforter and cutwork sheets and pillowcases. On the wall opposite the bed was a fireplace, flanked by two wing chairs, with a small mantel that held a collection of antique toys. The hardwood floors were covered by colorful hooked rugs in many shapes and sizes.

Casey pulled her clothes from her bag and tried to smooth the wrinkles with her trembling hands. Just the thought of spending the night with Matt in such a romantic setting was turning her into a nervous wreck. What would he expect of her? Would he act as though nothing had happened between them or would he pick up where they'd left off? Could she trust him?

A wave of apprehension filled her and she tried to bury the sudden feelings of clumsiness and inadequacy that undermined her earlier confidence.

Would she ever learn to trust again? There had been lies and deceptions in every relationship she had embarked on in the past. Larry the Lizard had a Mrs. Lizard lurking in the background. And there were the others—men for whom "I love you" was not an expression of deep commitment, but rather a synonym for "I want you." And for every failure, for every gullible acceptance of a lie, her confidence had been eroded a little more.

But she did have an advantage with Matt Garrison. She knew he would never proclaim his undying love for her—or any woman for that matter. So why not grab the opportunity he offered? A brief affair, sex without strings, a chance to rid herself of her anxieties and enjoy the act for once. She could take what she wanted and walk away.

She pulled open a door that she assumed led to a closet and was surprised to find a huge bathroom, complete with a deep whirlpool tub, a glass-block shower stall and stacks of soft white towels.

Without a second's thought she turned on the water in the tub, anxious to soak the cold from her bones and soothe her runaway nervousness. The house was silent. After their simple lunch of ham-and-cheese sandwiches, Matt had decided to venture out into the snow and explore the ranch. Ellen was curled up in the study, engrossed in a novel. A nice peaceful soak in the tub would be just what the doctor ordered.

Casey stripped off her clothes and pulled her hair up into a knot, then stepped gingerly into the steaming water and sank down into its glorious warmth. At her fingertips, she found a panel of buttons and pushed them individually, looking for the one that started the air jets in the tub. She laughed out loud when one button opened the draperies and revealed a floor-to-ceiling window with the same view as the bedroom. For all its rustic charm, the house was still pure Hollywood.

Closing her eyes, she leaned back and let the water rush around her. The heat made her drowsy. Tiny beads of perspiration dampened her face. Her eyelids felt heavy and she allowed her mind to drift and her body to relax.

She didn't know what prompted her to open her eyes, whether it was a sound or whether she sensed a presence in the room. But when she lazily turned her head toward the door she found him, arms crossed over his chest and a smile curving his lips.

"Mind if I join you?" Matt asked seductively, his voice teasing, almost demanding an impertinent or hostile answer.

She would not play this game with him anymore; she wouldn't let him intimidate her. Not after this morning. Things had changed between them and she wasn't going to pretend that they hadn't, no matter how hard he pretended otherwise. She was attracted to him. She wanted him. And maybe she was even falling in love with him. Hiding her needs behind a prickly facade would not make them magically disappear.

She smiled back, brushing a lock of hair from her damp cheek. "Suit yourself."

He looked at her in surprise and she was delighted by the fact that she had finally rendered Matt Garrison speechless. He could ply his charms on any willing woman, yet when the tables were turned, he couldn't handle it. He was all bark and no bite.

She watched as Matt's eyes moved down to the beads of water glittering on her shoulders and chest. He seemed to be fascinated as he watched the water bubble up around her breasts and chewed nervously on his lower lip, as if considering his next move.

"Well?" she asked. "Are you going to join me?"

Matt's attention snapped back to her face. "No . . . thanks. I just stopped in to see how you were doing. And to let you know that I'm going to take Jesse out for a ride before it starts snowing again. I came back to get my camera." He paused, staring at her as if he were considering changing his mind. "I left it in the bedroom," he added lamely.

"Like I said," Casey said, barely able to contain her amusement, "suit yourself." She closed her eyes and slid more deeply into the tub, listening to his movements in the bedroom.

She felt a tiny stab of disappointment as she heard the bedroom door close behind him. But her disappointment was quickly replaced by a sense of triumph. She had done it! Theodora would have been green with envy. She had scored a victory in the first battle of this dangerous but delicious war that they were waging between the two of them. And now she knew, without a doubt, that she had the power to beat Matt Garrison at his own game.

MATT SAT ON JESSE'S BACK, his face turned into the wind as his eyes scanned the western sky. Ominous gray clouds hovered over the mountaintops in the distance. The snow had stopped but there was more coming; he could feel it in the bite of the wind, could smell it in the damp, cold air. Reining Jesse sharply to the left, he turned and rode slowly back to the ranch house, trying to prolong his ride and put off the inevitable.

Though he had spent the last two hours in the cold, it hadn't done much to douse the fire burning inside him, a fire that had begun as a spark the day he and Casey had met. This morning it had turned into a flame. And when she had invited him into the tub this afternoon, the flame had exploded into a raging fire, as if someone had suddenly thrown gasoline on it.

At first, avoiding the heat she created inside him had been easy. She set his nerves on edge at every turn. And she was the one who had showed little interest in him as a man. Until she took things into her own hands.

Damn, it wasn't as if he didn't want her. He did. He wanted her more than he'd wanted any woman in a long time. He wanted her soft skin and her fragrant hair, her liquid green eyes and her full, lush lips. He wanted to feel his skin against hers, feel himself moving inside her.

*So why resist, Garrison? Take what she's offering. You've always taken it when it's been offered in the past. What's stopping you now?*

What *was* stopping him? Matt turned the question around in his mind. It had been so easy in the past—so many women, so many offers, and never a second thought, never an ounce of guilt. But out of nowhere, he had suddenly developed a conscience. A damn sense of honor.

He couldn't take her and then leave her. He knew that as soon as they made love, the ties that were forming between them would strengthen and tighten until he would be bound irrevocably to her, unable to leave, unable to live.

He cared about Casey; he respected her independence and her intelligence. And he didn't want to hurt her, something that was sure to happen if he let himself get involved with her. But she would want more than a casual affair. And he just didn't have what it took to make a commitment to a woman.

*Stay away from her, Garrison. She's dangerous. She'll tie you down. She'll take away your freedom.*

His decision was made. As soon as they got the story, he would leave. He would give her half the bonus and run. There would be no more deception and no guilt to plague him after he left.

Matt looked up at the windows that ran along the back of the ranch house, at the window of the bedroom he would share with Casey that night. In his mind he pictured her lying naked on the bed and he felt the flames of desire shoot through his body and heat his core.

With a groan of frustration, he kicked Jesse in the flanks and sent the huge horse bolting. He could evade her all he wanted during the day, but there would be no escaping her tonight.

IT WAS DARK WHEN CASEY woke from what she had intended to be a quick nap. She wandered toward the kitchen in her stocking feet and found Ellen, seated on a tall stool at the counter, carefully studying a thick cookbook. She looked up and smiled when Casey entered the room.

"Hi, " she said warmly, her blue eyes bright and friendly. "I'm glad you finally came down. I think I might need your help with dinner."

Casey pulled up a stool and plopped down beside her. The recipe was for quesadillas, a Mexican pizza that she had made many times.

"I'm afraid I'm not much of a cook," Ellen admitted. "David says it doesn't matter, that he loves me for my other qualities."

"David?"

"My fiancé, David Westfield. He's an attorney in New York. He was supposed to join me here this afternoon, but the blizzard messed up his flight plans. He should be here tomorrow afternoon if the weather clears." Casey watched Ellen's expression brighten as she spoke of her fiancé. "It's been nearly a month since I saw him last."

"Don't you live in New York, too?" she asked, struggling to ask the most logical questions, questions a total stranger might ask.

Ellen moved to assemble the ingredients for dinner on the counter and her voice took on a melancholy timbre. "No, I live in Los Angeles now. Though I plan to move to New York after we get married."

Casey's heart leaped at the sudden opening the conversation afforded her. "And when is that?" she asked nonchalantly.

"It was supposed to have been tomorrow morning. We planned on getting married here on the ranch, but with David's travel delay, I'm not sure what we'll do."

"That's too bad. It must be hard living so far away from the man you love," Casey commented.

"We've been apart for such a long time. We met when we were both in college at Northwestern. After college, we drifted in different directions, but a few years ago we met by chance in front of the Barrymore near the corner of West 47th and Broadway in New York City. I think it was fate that brought us back together. David says on an island the size of Manhattan, we were bound to meet sooner or later." Ellen laughed, a light-hearted girlish laugh. "David has a unique sense of humor. I think that's one of the things I love most about him. He always manages to make me laugh."

Casey felt a niggling sense of guilt tugging at her conscience. Why couldn't Ellen have been some self-absorbed starlet, aloof and pretentious, like so many other Hollywood celebrities? Instead of being snobbish, she was honest and sweet and giving, qualities Casey would find valuable in a good friend. For the first time since she decided to get this story, Casey realized that she might have to hurt someone in the process. She would have to betray the trust of a woman she was beginning to like very much.

"How long have you and Matt been married?"

"What?" Casey asked, hearing the question perfectly well, but needing extra time to come up with an answer.

"How long has it been, darlin'? Five years?" Casey stifled a sigh of relief as she noticed Matt standing in the doorway to the kitchen. The smooth planes of his face were ruddy with cold and his hair was windblown. He sat down on the empty stool beside her and gave her a chaste peck on the cheek. His lips, warm and firm, seemed to burn into her cheek and her mind immediately flashed back to a remembrance of him caressing her mouth with his tongue.

Casey jumped up from her stool and busied herself by pouring him a mug of coffee. "Where have you been?"

"I've been helping the ranch hands with their chores. I thought I'd do something to pay Ellen back for her hospitality."

Ellen smiled at him in gratitude. "You don't have to do that. You're my guest here."

Matt shrugged. "I enjoyed it. I don't get many chances to ride anymore. I'll take all the time on a horse I can get, especially on a horse like Jesse." Matt stretched his arms above his head, working the kinks out of his back. "Right now, I feel like *I've* been rode hard and put away wet."

Casey handed him the steaming mug of coffee, then crinkled her nose in disgust. "You smell like it, too."

Matt grabbed Casey around the waist and pulled her to him, playfully nuzzling his icy nose in the curve of her neck. She gently pushed him away, afraid to show how uncomfortable she felt wrapped in his arms and how truly repelled she was by the horsey odor that emanated from his clothing.

"All right, all right," Matt said, laughing and holding up his hands in mock surrender. "I won't offend your tender sensibilities any longer. I'll go take a shower."

"You better make it quick," Ellen called as he headed back to the bedroom. "With any luck, dinner will be ready in half an hour."

THEY ATE IN THE cozy study, the three of them sitting in front of a roaring fire. Matt had mixed up a batch of margaritas and after only a few sips, Casey felt warm and content, right down to the tips of her toes. A feeling of camaraderie enveloped them, as if they had been friends for many years, and they spoke of inconsequential things, laughing and joking with each other. Though Ellen avoided discussing her career, simply stating that she worked for one of the movie studios in Hollywood, Casey sensed that she felt uncomfortable dodging the truth.

When Ellen asked Matt about his photography, he regaled them with story after story of his exotic adventures. He sat next to Casey, his arm draped casually around her shoulders, as he spun funny and frightening tales.

His voice was smooth and expressive. He seemed to delight in the telling of a story and each adventure revealed a tiny piece of knowledge that Casey fit into the puzzle that made up Matt Garrison.

He told of the time he had saved a good friend of his who had been swept overboard from an Australian freighter during a storm in the South China Sea. He followed that story with one recounting the time he had been kidnapped by Pakistani rebels and forced to dig a bullet out of the leg of one of their leaders. "For some reason, they thought I was a doctor. I'd seen enough television to do a pretty good imitation, but I have no idea what they would have done to me if I'd have killed the guy."

"What about you, Casey? Don't you get a little frightened hearing about your husband's exploits?" Casey opened her mouth to answer Ellen's question, but Matt deftly steered the conversation back to him.

"I put those crazy days behind me the day I married Casey," he explained, squeezing her shoulder. "No more adventures for this guy. I find plenty to photograph here in the U.S."

"Do you go with Matt on all his assignments?" Ellen asked.

Once again, Matt jumped in. "I take Casey with me whenever I can."

"What do you do to occupy your time?" Ellen asked, firmly directing her question at Casey and frowning slightly at Matt's overbearing behavior.

Casey answered quickly before Matt had a chance to open his mouth. "I'm a writer," she blurted out. She felt Matt's fingers bite into the soft flesh of her arm. "I write detective novels." She knew his gaze was riveted on her.

Ellen studied her closely. "How interesting! Perhaps I've read one of your books."

"I haven't had anything published yet," Casey admitted, feeling her face color slightly. "But I hope to soon. I've completed two manuscripts and I'm working on a third. I've been rejected by more publishers than I care to count, but one of my manuscripts is with a publisher in New York right now. I haven't heard anything, but the way I see it, no news is good news."

As soon as the words had left her mouth, she regretted saying them. Her dream of becoming a novelist had been a closely held secret. But all Matt's talk about *his* life, his career, had prompted her to speak in her own defense. She had dreams and aspirations, too. And though she knew she could trust Ellen with them, she wasn't so sure she could trust Matt.

The thought of him knowing her innermost hopes and ambitions frightened her slightly. She felt susceptible and exposed around him. But that didn't stop her from wanting him or from needing him to want her.

Was it wicked, this obsession she seemed to have developed for Matt Garrison? Sex had never been of much interest to her before, but now it was all she could think about.

The conversation moved to other less personal subjects and Casey relaxed, enjoying the feel of Matt's arm around her shoulders and leaning into the warmth of his body. The heat from the fire and the effects of the tequila were beginning to make her drowsy and she felt her eyelids becoming heavier and her mind drifting off every now and then. Matt looked down at her as she hid a yawn with her hand.

"Ellen, I think I'd better get my wife to bed. She looks like she's falling asleep. And I have to admit, I'm a little beat myself. Riding with those ranch hands was hard work."

Matt stood up and reached for Casey's hand, pulled her up beside him and slipped his arm back around her shoulders. "Thank you for dinner and for your gracious company." He moved over to Ellen and kissed her lightly on the cheek. As Casey passed her, she took Ellen's hand, squeezed it and added her thanks.

As they made their way to their bedroom, her pulse began to race. All day long she had been both dreading and anticipating this moment. A wild jumble of emotions made her dizzy with paralyzing self-doubt and undeniable desire. Where would this night lead?

Casey knew exactly where she wanted it to lead. Right into Matt Garrison's arms. Then directly into his heart.

## 6

*I shouldn't have been surprised when I woke up alone, being all too familiar with his "kiss and run" tactics. Men. I've never claimed to understand them, but that hasn't stopped me from trying. I had seen this guy stare down the business end of a gun barrel more times than I could count, without showing an ounce of fear. Yet, the prospect of waking up in the same bed with me seemed to scare him out of his wits. I knew he had searched my apartment while I slept. I also knew he hadn't found what he was after. Well, at least one of us got what we were looking for last night.*

*Men. Who can figure?*

SHE HAD REREAD the paragraph countless times, her eyes taking in the words, but her mind failing to register their meaning. Instead, her thoughts were occupied with Matt's unfathomable behavior. With a groan of frustration, Casey slapped her notebook shut and threw it in the direction of her open tote bag, then tossed her glasses on the bedside table. She snuggled down beneath the fluffy comforter and hugged a pillow to her chest.

Somewhere between the back seat of the truck and the bedroom door, something had happened. The arrogantly confident and irritatingly sexy Matt Garrison had been kidnapped and a bewildering twin left in his place. He suddenly seemed intent on avoiding her—her glances, her touch, her presence.

Lord, he was behaving as if she'd suddenly contracted the plague! Mumbling some excuse about finding somewhere else to sleep, he had left her standing at the bedroom door. What was he afraid of? She was the one who should have been nervous. He was the one with all the experience, Mr. "Love-'Em-And-Leave-'Em."

Casey tried to sort out Matt's motivations in her mind. From the beginning he had teased her and taunted her, his words always spoken with seductive undertones. Finally she had taken up the subtle challenge and returned his advances in full measure. When she had initiated the seduction in the truck he had been a willing participant. Then there was his comment about joining her in the bath. And all evening he had been warm and attentive.

What had caused him to shy away from entering the bedroom with her? Could he sense her apprehension? Had he taken that for a lack of desire on her part? Or was his behavior earlier that evening just an act, for Ellen's sake?

Over and over, she ran the scenes through her mind. Even if he thought she was just another willing female susceptible to his charms, just another woman throwing herself at him, why would he resist?

But he was resisting now, Casey thought. He had built a veritable stone wall between them in the course of just a few moments. Why?

*Because he doesn't want to hurt your feelings, you dimwit!*

*Because he's afraid of the feelings you stir up inside him.*

*He's got a communicable disease.*

*No, he's in love with someone else.*

*He's married?*

*Stop it, stop it, stop it,* her mind shrieked. She muffled a scream with the downy-soft pillow and kicked her feet in frustration beneath the heavy covers.

*Damn you, Matt Garrison! Quit messing with my life.* She jerked herself upright, pushed the pillow to the floor and swept her rumpled hair from her eyes, then jumped out of bed and began to pace the room.

As her anger calmed, she slowed her steps and wandered aimlessly about, picking up the antique toys from the mantelpiece and examining them one by one. She walked past Matt's backpack several times, and each time paused slightly to peer into the top before moving to another spot in the room. But her innate curiosity got the better of her and she soon found herself sitting on the floor, casually picking through his possessions.

She knew so little about him. He carried his professional life in his camera bag, but his personal life he carried in his backpack. Maybe his belongings would give her a clue to his behavior. *And maybe with a little more time I can come up with a better excuse for being nosy,* she scolded herself.

She pulled out a soft buff-colored shirt and held it up to her nose, then closed her eyes and inhaled his scent. So much like the wind and rain, so fresh and clean and smelling faintly of his cologne. Burying her face in the fabric, she allowed her mind to conjure up visions of him, disturbingly sexy images of dark hair and smoky blue eyes, warm lips and hard muscle. Casey pulled off her long cotton sleep shirt, slipped her arms into the long sleeves of his shirt and drew it around her naked body.

An address book near the bottom of the pack caught her eye and she pulled it out and flipped through the pages, counting the names of the women she came across. By the time she reached the letter *R* she had lost count. So there had been a lot of women. What had she expected?

After carefully repacking his belongings, she realized that she had forgotten to replace his shirt. But taking it off was forgotten the instant she spied his shaving kit nestled against the wall behind the backpack. She grabbed the leather bag and walked over to the bed, her mind engrossed in an inventory of the contents: his toothbrush, his razor, a tube of toothpaste, a bar of soap. Every item was carefully examined before she tossed it onto the bed and went on to the next. She opened his cologne, brought the bottle to her nose and sniffed, then dabbed it on her wrists.

A small box at the bottom of the kit caught her attention and she pulled it out, then threw the leather bag onto the bed. The box of condoms shouldn't have caught her by surprise. Most single men probably carried the same protection. But the thought of Matt purchasing and using them brought an uncomfortable blush to her cheeks.

A box of twelve, she mused as she pulled the top flap open and peeked inside. How long would that last him?

A year? A month? Maybe a week? She dumped the foil packages into her hand and tried to count them, wondering how many he had already used. She had nearly finished when she heard the bedroom door open. Her breath stopped in her throat as she glanced up and saw him standing at the open door, watching her, one eyebrow raised in question.

A wave of heat washed over her. She had been caught snooping. Quickly, she tried to push the suddenly enormous packages into the now miniscule box. But her fingers fumbled the task and the condoms scattered around her feet like leaves dropping from a tree. With a tiny yelp, she bent down to gather them up, and hastily stuffed them back into the box, keeping her desperate gaze on the floor.

The toes of his boots came into her field of view just as she closed the box. Slowly she let her eyes drift upward. She watched as he bent to retrieve an overlooked package. He held the condom in front of her nose.

"You forgot one," he said, the corners of his mouth quivering as he tried to contain his grin.

She snatched the package from his grasp. Damn, why was there never a hole handy when she needed one? A huge gaping crater, where she could hide her entire mortified body.

"I—I was looking for a—a pencil," she stammered, hoping to salvage at least some of her dignity with an excuse.

"That's certainly the first place *I'd* look," he said in mock seriousness.

Slowly he reached down to her, brushing his hand past her cheek. She felt him touch her ear and her heart sank to her toes. He pulled at the pencil she had tucked behind her ear and held it out to her.

She snatched it from his fingers. "Thanks," she mumbled, "I was wondering where that went."

Casey stood up and hurried to the bed where she gathered the contents of his shaving kit and returned everything to the leather bag. When she finished the task, she walked stiffly across the room, avoiding his gaze, and put the kit back where she had found it. In a few quick steps she was back in bed, the covers pulled up around her neck.

He studied her for a moment, then shook his head and laughed. She wanted to scream. The whole incident seemed to be vastly amusing to him. Well, it certainly wasn't funny to her! Why did he always manage to catch her at her worst? He turned and walked to the fireplace.

"So what do you think of this house?" His voice was casual, the question innocuous but still laced with suppressed humor. "It belongs to J. D. Latimer, the producer of Ellen's last movie."

"Is that so?" Casey answered, her voice betraying her embarrassment.

An uncomfortable silence pervaded the room. Casey smoothed the surface of the comforter and picked nervously at a tiny thread. "I thought you were going to find somewhere else to sleep."

"I was," he said turning to her, "but then I decided we'd better talk. Something happened this morning that neither one of us was prepared for."

Oh, she might not have been prepared, but he certainly was! Twelve? He was prepared for more than just a morning in a snowbound truck; he was prepared for an entire week. "Forget it," she shot back defensively. "It was a mistake. Let's not make another mistake by talking about it."

"I didn't think—"

"And neither did I. I don't want to discuss it, Garrison. Let's just pretend it never happened."

"If that's what you want," he said with a scowl. He took a deep breath, then let it out slowly. Casey could almost see the relief flooding his features and she felt her anger swell.

*Don't worry, Matt Garrison. I wouldn't think of forcing my attentions on you.*

He busied himself building a fire in the fireplace. To paper and kindling he added several pieces of wood, then set the whole thing ablaze. "Did you find out anything else about Ellen's boyfriend?"

"Like what?" Casey asked, unable to keep her irritation in check.

He threw her an exasperated look, as if she were some recalcitrant child he was forced to look after. "What do women usually talk about when they're together? Did she say anything else?"

"Yes." Casey felt like baiting him, like drawing him into an argument. It would give her the opportunity to tell him exactly what she thought of him.

"Well, are you going to tell me or are you just going to sit there sulking for the rest of the night?"

"She told me about David, that's her fiancé. She told me how they met and how she loved his sense of humor. And she told me how much she missed him and how they planned to live in New York after they were married."

A satisfied smile stole across his lips. "You did well, Carmichael, gaining her confidence like that. What about the wedding?"

Casey shook her head, composing herself carefully before sidestepping the truth. "Nothing," she answered. "Garrison, I'm beginning to get a bad feeling about this whole thing. I don't like deceiving her."

"She's not your friend, Carmichael. She's the subject of your story. *Our* story. Don't start to get soft on me now."

"Whether she's my friend or not makes no difference. It just doesn't seem right, that's all."

"Listen, we've got a chance at a real blockbuster here, and I emphasize the word real. You don't have to make this one up. No more UFOs and Elvis sightings. This is real journalism now."

"I've never made a story up! It's unethical."

"Give me a break," he cried, flopping down into one of the wing chairs. "The tabloids do it all the time and they'll continue to do it until it doesn't sell papers anymore. You and I both know that unless the courts can prove malicious intent, the scandal sheets can write whatever they want about whomever they want."

"And you don't think we're being malicious? Lying our way into this house, pretending to be something we aren't, taking the happiest day of a woman's life and holding it up for public inspection just to give everyone something to gossip about over the watercooler at work?"

"This story is worth twenty-five thousand dollars. Have you forgotten that very important fact? My scruples disappear around the one-hundred-dollar level," he answered sarcastically. "If you want to back out now, that's fine. But don't expect me to share your misplaced loyalties. When Ellen Hansen became Emily Harrington, she gave up her right to privacy. That's what being a celebrity means, Carmichael. It means people recognize you and listen to you and want to know your every move. If we don't write this story, someone else will, and then it probably will be a total fabrication."

"I know that," Casey conceded. "It doesn't make it any easier. I just don't like lying."

"You're not lying. You're telling the readers the truth, for once."

"Don't try to twist my words. You know what I mean."

"All right, if it makes you that uncomfortable, then back out."

"That would make you happy, wouldn't it," she snapped. "Well, forget it. I'm not backing out."

He pushed his long, lean frame out of the wing chair and came to stand in front of her. His eyes followed the outline of her body under the blankets on the bed. "Good. Now I think we better both get some sleep. Tomorrow is going to be a busy day."

Matt moved to the bed, unbuttoned his plaid flannel shirt and let it drop to the floor behind him. Casey watched the light from the fire dancing across the smooth contours of his chest and the rippled muscles of his stomach, then quickly quelled the flood of desire that raced through her body. He sat down on the end of the bed and tugged off his boots and socks, then reached up to pull down the covers.

Casey snatched the covers from his hands, leaned over and gave him a level look. "When hell freezes over," she warned. "And not a day sooner."

The corners of his mouth turned up in a familiar, challenging smile. The game between them had resumed. "Where do you suggest I sleep?"

"You're a smart guy. You figure it out."

Matt tugged at the covers again, but when Casey remained adamant, he reluctantly climbed off the bed and retrieved his sleeping bag from among the possessions he had scattered around their room. He wrapped it around his wide shoulders, returned to the wing chair and pulled the other chair closer to cradle his bare feet. When she saw he was settled, she flipped off the bedside lamp. The room was plunged into shadow, lit only by the wavering orange glow of the fire.

"Hey, Carmichael," he called softly. "I like that shirt you're wearing. I've got one just like it."

ONE ... TWO ... THREE ... four ... five. Somewhere in the silent depths of the ranch house, a clock chimed. Matt counted each strike of the bell as he had done every hour for the past three hours. His eyes were fixed on the dwindling light from the fire, and he watched the embers pulsating with blue and orange lights. He rubbed his eyes then glanced back down at the notebook that lay open on his lap.

Casey was a helluva writer, he thought, as he ran a finger tenderly along the precisely written lines. She wrote with a humorous, tongue-in-cheek wit, engaging the reader from the very first paragraph and weaving a mystery filled with inventive twists and turns. Her words flowed across the page in one continuous strand, unbroken by scribbled-out phrases and smudged erasures. If this was her first draft, he wondered how her second would read.

It angered him that her talent hadn't been recognized. He knew how it felt to have work so painstakingly conceived be ignored by those who might legitimize it. He had grown immune to the rejection of his own work, but it was surprisingly hard to accept the rejection of Casey's work.

He threw an arm across his eyes and sighed in frustration. When had her feelings become so important to him? From the moment he had met her, he'd known she was someone special. He had never really intended to trick and deceive her. He could never hurt her. And he didn't want to see her hurt.

He stood and tossed a fresh log on top of the charred remains of another, sending a shower of sparks scattering across the hearth, then glanced over at the sleeping figure on the bed. As if drawn by some unseen force, he found himself standing over her, watching the even rise and fall of her chest as she slept.

She was curled up on her side, her hands pressed together under her cheek like a child. Her auburn hair, fanned across the pillow, shimmered with golden highlights from the fire. His fingers itched with the need to burrow through the tangled curls and he rubbed his palms together to quell the impulse.

He let his mind drift back to that morning, to the feel of her flesh beneath his fingers, and the tiny sounds of pleasure she had made when he touched her. ger, deep and aching, pulsed through his body.

How had she done it, this sweetly vulnerable woman? How had she managed to capture his soul in just a few short days? Before her, it had been easy to leave, to move on from job to job with no regrets and no strings attached. But he knew, no matter how much distance might come between them, she would still invade his thoughts.

Suddenly, he found himself thinking of her as part of his future. In his mind, he had already mapped out his next adventure, his trip to Chile, and he wondered if he could take her along. Would she agree to come with him? Or would she be content to wait in Los Angeles until he returned?

He was tempted to lay all his cards on the table, to tell her how he felt, but something held him back. A commitment to her would put an end to his life as he knew it. He would be responsible for someone other than himself. Decisions would be made between the two of them; his life would no longer belong entirely to him. It was much simpler to be selfish, much easier to be responsible for just himself.

Matt knelt down next to the bed, carefully rested his elbows on the mattress and moved closer to study her features in the glow of the fire. He picked up a curl from the pillow and rubbed it between his thumb and forefinger, trying to memorize the silken feel of it, knowing he would want to recall it at another, more solitary time.

His fingers moved closer to her face, and hovered above the smooth, alabaster contour of her cheek. He knew he risked waking her, but the need to touch her warm skin was too great to deny. Slowly he ran the tip of his index finger down her jawline, tracing the shape of her chin. His thumb moved to caress her lower lip and he remembered the soft, sensual feel of her mouth on his.

She stirred slightly, turning her head away from his hand and parting her lips in a sleepy sigh. Without thinking, he bent over and gently kissed her. Just one kiss would have to satisfy his undeniable craving for her. He could let it go no further.

Though he was certain of the pleasure he could give her, and even more sure of the pleasure she would give him, he also knew he could never give her what she truly wanted and needed. He couldn't stay, and she deserved someone who would.

But he would give her something worthwhile before they parted ways. He would give her her dream.

CASEY OPENED HER EYES to the dim light of dawn filtering through the windows of the bedroom. As her eyes became accustomed to the light, she saw him watching her intently from a chair he had pulled up beside the bed.

"What time is it?" she asked, noticing that he was fully dressed.

He spoke without taking his eyes from hers, his voice soft and soothing. "It's early. Go back to sleep."

The gently spoken words calmed her and she relaxed into the encompassing warmth of the bed, smiling drowsily up at him. It was nice to wake up to him in the morning, to have him near. "What are you doing?"

"Looking at you."

"Why?"

He reached out to touch her cheek with his fingertips. Casey felt a current of desire pass from his fingers through her body. "Because, someday, I'll be sitting in some sleazy bar in Bangkok, surrounded by even sleazier women, and I'll want to remember what you look like, so warm and soft from sleep. I'm taking a mental photograph so I'll never forget you."

Casey drew herself up on one elbow and looked at him suspiciously. His words sounded so sincere. An arrow of pain pierced her heart at the thought of them being apart, but her mistrust quickly returned. What kind of game was he playing now? Was he teasing her or making fun of her? She laughed lightly, but the sound seemed forced. "I would think, after all we've been through, you'd just as soon forget me," she said, her breath catching in her throat.

He shook his head and smiled. "No. I think that would be impossible." He paused to clear his throat uncomfortably. "A man doesn't just forget a woman like you." He studied her expression closely, then pushed himself reluctantly out of the chair and looked down at her. "I'll never forget you, Casey," he muttered, his voice cracking slightly. "I promise you that."

Then he turned, walked to the door and pulled it closed behind him without looking back.

"And I won't forget you, Matt Garrison," she whispered to herself as she stared at the door.

She kept her eyes fixed on the door long after he had gone, silently willing him to return. He wanted her, she was almost certain of it now. But what was holding him back? Why was he suddenly determined to stay out of her bed? And what could she do to change his mind?

She rolled to her side and pulled the covers up to her nose, hoping to fall back asleep. But several minutes later she sat up in bed and wiped the final traces of slumber from her eyes. The wood floor felt cold on her bare feet as she stepped from the bed.

When she pushed the wing chair back to its spot near the fireplace, she noticed her notebook, caught between the cushion and the arm of the chair. What was it doing there? Had she left it on the chair last night? She pulled it out and flipped through the pages but noticed nothing out of place. Her actions of the previous night came back to her clearly. She had thrown the book on top of her tote bag.

Casey sat down in the chair, clutching the notebook to her chest. He had read her manuscript. That's why his eyes had looked so red and tired. He had spent the night reading her book! No one had ever read one of her manuscripts, no one except the faceless editors in New York.

Yet somehow, the thought of Matt reading her book didn't really bother her. They had developed a friendship, tenuous as it might be, and she could count on him to be brutally honest. He would tell her exactly what he thought of her writing.

So why hadn't he said anything? She thought back to their odd, stilted conversation. He seemed so preoccupied, so distant, as if his thoughts troubled him.

Had he found her writing that bad? Or maybe it was something else. Could he be having the same doubts about pursuing the story as she had?

The more time she spent with Ellen, the harder it was to separate Emily, the movie star, from Ellen, the woman. No one deserved to have their private life trumpeted in large type at newsstands and grocery store checkouts, not even someone who deliberately chose the life of a celebrity.

But this story was her only chance to get the five thousand dollars she needed for the down payment. To Emily, it was small change, a new dress, a weekend vacation. But to Casey, it meant roots, a long-awaited return to a place she loved. She was no different from Matt, footloose and fancy-free, without a real home, without ties. But Matt had chosen that life for himself. She had been pushed into it when she was forced to sell her grandparents' home to pay back taxes and funeral expenses. She had been so young when it all happened.

Losing the house had been like snipping the string of a kite. For Matt, it would have meant soaring free, the chance to fly high above the more unfortunate earthbound, to see sights reserved for only a special few. But for Casey, the string was a connection to those she loved, a tie to her past, a guide for her future. She could still blow about in the wind, twisting and dipping, but she could also come gently back to earth and relish the quiet solitude of being home.

She deserved to have some contentment in her life. She deserved to realize her dreams. Emily had dealt with the tabloids before and would deal with them many more times in the future. Emily was Ellen, and Ellen was Emily, after all. They were one and the same person. Matt was right. If they didn't report this story, someone else would.

With a renewed sense of determination, Casey grabbed her notebook and turned to a clean page. Curling up in the wing chair, she began to write, the words rushing from her mind onto the paper. But she didn't write Theodora's story. Instead, she began the story of Emily Ellen Harrington Hansen and the Hollywood wedding of the year.

Her dream was almost within her grasp. She would reach out and grab it. She wouldn't let it get away.

## 7

*The bank manager placed the narrow steel box on the table in front of me. I waited until he left the room before I opened it and examined the contents. The address book was hidden beneath several bundles of hundred-dollar bills. I flipped through the pages, my heart freezing as I recognized name after name. Once the police got hold of the book, hundreds of lives would be irreparably damaged. Yet all I needed to solve this murder was one name out of hundreds in the damn book. As I walked out of the bank with the book tucked under my arm, two questions swam in my mind.*

*Could I nail the murderer with the book? And could I live with myself if I did? There were no easy answers.*

CASEY SHOVED her notebook into the bottom of her tote bag and covered it carefully with layers of clothes. She had been up since 6:00 a.m., pacing her room, scribbling in her notebook and waiting impatiently for Ellen to awaken. Her watch read ten o'clock when the smell of coffee drew her to the kitchen.

Ellen was peering intently through the window of the oven when Casey padded in. "Morning," Ellen muttered distractedly.

"Good morning, Ellen." Casey moved behind her to pour herself a cup of coffee, then sat down on one of the breakfast stools and waited for Ellen to join her. But Ellen continued her intense perusal of the interior of the oven, glancing up every few seconds to study the automatic timer. When the buzzer went off, she opened the oven door, pulled out a muffin pan and slid it carefully onto the counter.

She stared down at the pan of misshapen muffins and reached out to poke the surface of one with her index finger. Then without any warning, she burst into tears, grabbed the hot pan and threw it toward the sink. The muffins flew across the counter and onto the floor. Ripping the oven mitt off her right hand, she sent it sailing across the kitchen.

"I can't do this," she sobbed, sliding to the floor and disappearing below the edge of the counter. "I just can't."

Casey jumped off her stool and rushed behind the counter to find Ellen with her face buried in her knees and her arms clasped tightly around her legs. Casey dropped down beside her, put her arm around her and patted her shoulder consolingly. Ellen lifted her tear-streaked face and looked at Casey, then burst into a fresh round of tears.

"I—I can't even cook," she said between wrenching sobs. "I don't know wh-wh-why he wants to ma-ma-marry me."

Casey wrapped her other arm around Ellen and hugged her. "He wants to marry you," she explained in a soothing voice, "because he loves you more than anything else in this whole wide world. More than himself. More than...life itself. And much, much more than muffins."

Ellen looked up at Casey, her watery eyes wide with surprise. A tiny smile tugged at her lips, then grew wider and wider until she burst into a fit of uncontrollable laughter. Her laughter was infectious and soon Casey found herself giggling as hard as Ellen, as they sprawled on the kitchen floor, their backs against the cabinets.

"I'm such a dope," Ellen stammered between fresh gales of laughter.

Casey looked at her and nodded. "Yes," she answered soberly, "I would have to agree with you there. As far as I know, bad muffins don't rank very high on the list of reasons for divorce." This started another round of laughter. Ellen picked up a muffin and threw it at Casey but missed her head by inches. When the muffin bounced off the refrigerator door and landed back at Ellen's feet, they both completely lost control and rolled onto the tile floor clutching their stomachs.

"I made these for our honeymoon breakfast," Ellen gasped between giggles.

"The honeymoon will be over before it's even begun. And you'll be a widow if you let David eat these." Casey picked up a pair of muffins and knocked them together.

Ellen took a deep breath and brought her giggles under control, then sighed. "Thank you," she said, struggling to sit up. She looked sheepishly at Casey. "I've been such a nervous wreck this entire week."

Casey sat up beside her. "All brides go through the same thing." She had heard the comment somewhere and it sounded good to her.

"Did you?"

Casey felt a sharp pang of guilt. "Yes, I did." Afraid to let Ellen delve into her married state any further, she changed the subject. "Why don't we start over with the muffins?" she suggested. "I mastered muffins a few years ago, so I'll teach you what I know."

They crawled around on the floor and gathered up the scattered evidence of Ellen's baking abilities. Dirty bowls filled the sink and Casey began to rinse them and place them in the dishwasher. As she worked, she noticed Ellen standing silently beside her, an indecisive look on her face. She opened her mouth to speak, then smiled at Casey and began to play nervously with a set of measuring spoons.

"I know we've only known each other a few days," she began as if she were choosing her words very carefully. "But I want to thank you for being my friend. I don't have many true friends." Ellen paused, then her words began to rush out. "Casey, I want to tell you something that I hope you won't be angry about. It has to do with my job. The reason I don't have many real friends has to do with my job. I'm . . ."

"I know," Casey said softly. "You're Emily Harrington."

"H-how did you know?"

"I recognized you the first time I saw you."

"But you didn't say anything."

"I thought that if you wanted us to know, you would have told us."

"And it doesn't make any difference to you? It always makes such a difference," Ellen said sadly.

"Of course not. I'll always think of you as Ellen Hansen."

Ellen smiled in relief. "You don't know how much that means to me. There are days when I'd do anything to escape Emily's life. And I will soon. After I'm through with this next movie, I'm leaving California for good. I'm moving to New York and I'm going to do theater and bake cookies and have babies. I'm going to be Ellen Hansen again."

Joy radiated from Ellen's face. It was as if she were contemplating freedom after years and years of captivity. Ellen Hansen was nothing more than a prisoner in Emily Harrington's life.

"It's been horrible, these last few years. Ever since I fell in love with David, I've wanted to get out. But so many people count on me."

"So you're just going to quit?" Casey asked.

"It sounds complicated," Ellen explained, "but after I made the decision, it really wasn't. Two years ago, I started turning down offers. My agent is beside himself, my business manager has developed an ulcer, and my box office has never been better. And do you know what? I don't care!" Ellen laughed. "I have one more picture to finish and then I'm through with it all. I'm through with letting other people run my life."

"Is it really that bad?" Casey asked.

"Marriage is difficult enough without all the baggage that comes with a Hollywood wife," Ellen explained as she sifted flour into a bowl. "I just can't do that to David. The lack of privacy, the long separations, the plastic life-style. David isn't used to having his life examined under a microscope. And I've never gotten used to it. You know, they even go through my garbage."

"They?" Casey asked, already knowing the answer.

"The reporters," Ellen explained. "They stand at the end of my driveway every Thursday morning and pick through my garbage. Can you imagine making a living off someone's garbage? And let me tell you, it's a real pain to have to watch what I throw away."

"I can imagine," Casey said in a choked voice, guilt threatening to suffocate her.

"I just hope that David and I will be as happy as you and Matt are."

Casey began to put the other ingredients for the muffins into the bowl in front of Ellen, anxious to move the conversation in a different direction. "It's not all a bed of roses. Marriage would be a near perfect state, if it weren't for those damn husbands," Casey said flippantly.

"But Matt adores you!"

"What?"

"Oh, he does. The way he looks at you when you're not looking. It's all right there in his eyes. He is one hundred percent, absolutely, totally in love with you."

Casey looked at Ellen, trying to hide her shock. Matt in love with her? That was crazy! It was all just an act, a charade for Ellen's sake. But Ellen was a trained actress; if anyone could spot an act, she could. Where had she gotten such an absurd idea?

"Yes...well...why don't we get started on these muffins?" Casey stammered, her thoughts preoccupied with Ellen's startling revelation. "The key to good muffins is not to overmix—"

"Hello!" An unfamiliar male voice echoed through the front hallway. "Anybody home? Ellen, are you here?"

At the sound of the voice, Ellen jumped from her stool with a whoop of delight, scampered to the doorway of the kitchen and threw herself into the arms of a tall, blond man. Casey knew immediately that David Westfield had arrived when the laughing pair clung to each other and lost themselves in a passionate kiss.

They made a stunning couple; David's fair hair and blue eyes contrasted sharply with Ellen's dark hair and eyes. His elegant cashmere topcoat and finely tailored suit made him look out of place beside Ellen, who was dressed in faded jeans and a ragged sweatshirt. The New York attorney and the Hollywood actress. An odd couple by Hollywood standards. But Casey could sense immediately that they were meant for each other.

Ellen turned back to Casey, her face flushed, and made the introductions breathlessly. "David, this is Casey Garrison. Casey, my fiancé, David Westfield." Ellen immediately looked back at David as if she needed to assure herself that he was really there. "Casey and her husband Matt have been keeping me company. Their truck went off the road during the blizzard and they've been staying here until they can get it out."

David held out his hand to Casey, keeping one arm firmly around Ellen's shoulders. "Casey, it's a pleasure to meet you. I met your husband and some of the ranch hands down on the road as I was driving in. The tow truck had just arrived."

"What took you so long?" Ellen asked, hugging him even more tightly around his narrow waist. "You were supposed to be here an hour ago."

"I had a reporter tailing me. It took me an hour at the Denver airport to shake him."

Ellen's smile faded and bitterness crept into her voice. "Why can't they leave us alone?"

David kissed her on the forehead, then looked into her eyes. "It's all right. I bought another ticket and got on a plane for L.A. He followed me, and I managed to get off at the last minute with the help of a very accommodating flight attendant. The creep is now on his way to Los Angeles, where I'm sure he'll find someone else to bother."

"Are you sure?" she asked, the hurt and distrust still evident in her voice.

"Positive."

Casey felt a rush of overwhelming guilt as she listened to the conversation. Though she had walked into the kitchen determined to get her story, deep down inside she knew her decision had already been made. She couldn't betray Ellen's trust. She couldn't hurt her in such a callous way. Her grandparents had raised her to be honest. In the past few days she had done more lying and deceiving than she had ever done in her entire life.

She would give up the story and she would give up her dream. And now that the decision was made, there was only one problem. How to convince Matt to give up.

Ellen smiled up at her fiancé, basking in the warmth of his nearness. Then she stood on tiptoe and whispered something into his ear. He turned to look at her. "If that's what you want, it's fine with me," he said affectionately.

"Casey, David and I would like you and Matt to stay for our wedding. We'll understand if you have to leave, but it would mean a lot to us if you'd serve as our witnesses. The justice of the peace will be here tomorrow morning at ten."

"I—I don't know, Ellen," Casey answered. Her only hope of convincing Matt to leave was to convince him there would be no wedding. If he knew a wedding was imminent, getting him to leave would be impossible. "Matt is already late for an important photo assignment. He's anxious to get back on the road as soon as he can."

"Please, it would mean so much to have someone here. We couldn't invite our families. The reporters would have been right behind them."

"I'll ask Matt," Casey said softly. "But I really don't think we can stay."

"I'm sure you can convince him," Ellen said with a smile. "Now if you'll excuse us, I would like to get reacquainted with my future husband. I'm afraid you and Matt will have to fend for yourselves this evening, Casey. We'll see you tomorrow morning." Ellen grabbed David's hand and began to drag him in the direction of her bedroom, laughing at the flush of embarrassment that crept up his cheeks.

CASEY FOUND MATT STANDING in the driveway with his head underneath the hood of the Blazer. He looked up as she approached and smiled at her, a brief glimmer of desire in his eyes. He opened his mouth to speak, but she quickly jumped in, afraid of hearing explanations for his earlier behavior.

"Garrison, we have to talk."

"I know," he answered. Casey watched as he reached underneath the hood and began to turn a wing nut on the top of the engine. "The groom has arrived. I saw him drive in. Any idea if they're going to tie the knot in the near future?" He turned back to her, the wing nut and a large, round cover in his hands.

"What are you doing?" she asked, deftly ignoring his question.

"I'm buying some time. Here, hold this," he said as he handed her what she thought was the air-cleaner cover. He quickly turned back to the truck.

"Garrison, what are you doing?" she repeated more insistently as she stepped closer to the truck and peered under the hood.

"It's called sabotage, Carmichael. I'm making sure we can't leave today. See this pink wire. This is the ignition wire." Matt gave a quick tug on the wire, then held up the disconnected end to show her. "With this disconnected, we can't start the truck. Now I just have to put the air cleaner back on and we'll be all set."

Casey shook her head in amazement, momentarily distracted from her purpose. "Where did you learn how to do that?"

"Don't ask. Let's just say the skill has come in handy on more than one occasion."

"And what happens when we want to leave?"

"I just reconnect the wire and away we go."

"Well, reconnect it right now," she said. "I want to get out of here."

Matt slammed down the hood of the truck, then spun around to face her with a look of disbelief. "I thought we settled this last night. We're not leaving until we get what we came here for."

"I don't care about the story or the money!" The words rushed from her lips all at once. "If you don't agree to leave right now, I'm going to tell them the truth. I can't lie anymore."

Casey could see a brief flare of anger gleaming in Matt's eyes, but he quickly snuffed it out and smiled persuasively. "Casey, we went through all this last night. You agreed to stick with the story. We're so close. We had an agreement."

"Fix the ignition, Garrison," Casey ordered, turning to climb into the truck. "We're leaving." She slammed the driver's-side door of the Blazer and turned the key that Matt had left in the ignition. Matt watched her, a knowing smirk on his face. The truck refused to start.

She grabbed the keys from the ignition, jumped out and began walking toward the ranch house.

"Where are you going?" Matt shouted after her.

"I'm going to find one of the ranch hands. Someone should know how to get this truck started."

"Carmichael, give me those keys. We're not leaving." Matt ran after her, but Casey saw him coming and increased her pace, heading for the relative safety of the house. In three long strides he caught her, grabbed her around the waist and picked her up off her feet.

"Give me those keys," he demanded, grabbing for the hand she held outstretched to evade his.

She wriggled and turned, trying to break his hold. "No," she said with a scream. "David and Ellen have a right to their privacy. It's a basic human right outlined in the Constitution."

"Give me the keys!"

"No," Casey shouted, wrenching her arm back. She thought she had a firm grip on the key ring, but suddenly they were flying through the air. Matt dropped her to the ground and they both watched as the keys sank silently into a snowdrift ten feet away.

They turned to each other, then looked at the snowdrift. In a mad scramble of skidding feet and flying snow they launched themselves at the drift, burrowing through the three feet of snow in a frantic search for the keys.

Casey found them first and clutched them in her hand. But Matt pushed her back into the snow, flopped on top of her and reached for her hand. She squirmed beneath him, throwing snow at him with her free hand and kicking her legs. When he straddled her waist, she knew she was trapped.

"We had an agreement," he said, pinning her arm in the snow. "Celebrities are fair game."

"I don't care who Ellen is or what career choice she made," Casey shot back breathlessly. "She deserves to be happy." She grabbed a handful of snow and threw it at his face.

"And what about you?" he said, his voice soft with well-controlled anger. He pulled the keys from her grasp. "You deserve to be happy. The money from this story could give you the security to work on your novel full-time. Casey, you deserve that. You're a good writer, you have talent."

Matt stared down at her, his hair and face coated with snow. Then in one smooth movement, he lowered his head and captured her mouth. She didn't protest, but went limp at the touch of his tongue against hers. Sliding his legs along hers, he moved to cover her body and pulled her on top of him. They rolled back and forth in the snow, trying to deepen the kiss, trying to feel each other through the layers of sodden clothing.

Matt pulled open the front of her jacket and caressed her breasts through the bulky knit of her sweater. Casey ripped off her mittens and ran her hands through his damp hair, then turned his mouth against hers as he teased at her tongue.

The sounds of whistling and clapping brought them back to reality. Casey pulled away from Matt and struggled to sit up when she heard his name being called. Matt rolled over and sat up next to her, and they both came face-to-face with an audience of four ranch hands, howling and clapping and shouting their encouragement.

"Way to go, Garrison."

"Keep the little lady in line."

"Don't let her wear the pants in the family."

Casey's blush of embarrassment was replaced by fury when Matt pulled her to her feet and into his arms, and kissed her soundly. The ranch hands increased their applause until Casey jerked away and ran toward the house.

"You had no right to read my notebook," she shouted over her shoulder.

He caught up with her in a few long strides, took her elbow and drew her to a stop. She kept her eyes fixed on the front door on the house and refused to look at him. "But I did read it. And you are talented. You deserve this, Casey. You deserve to be happy."

Was he really more concerned about her happiness than his share of the bonus? Or was he simply trying to get her to agree to his way of thinking? Casey pulled away and continued toward the house. "Not at the expense of Ellen Hansen," she shouted. She hurried into the house, and walked quickly back to the bedroom, but she knew escape from him would be impossible.

She was standing near the bed when he entered the room and closed the door firmly behind him. He stalked up to her and picked up their argument without pause. "What about me?" he said, keeping his voice low and even. "Why don't I get a share of this valuable Carmichael loyalty? Or is that only reserved for people you care about?"

Casey detected the pain in his voice and felt the need to reassure him. "I care about you," she said softly, reaching out to caress his cheek. "I truly do. But neither you nor I need this money. We'll both survive without it. We're born survivors, you and I. We can roll with the punches. But Ellen is more fragile. She's fighting against pretty tough odds to make her marriage work. I won't be responsible for causing her pain."

Matt closed his eyes and stood silently, his mouth tight with anger. Slowly she pulled her hand away. He opened his eyes and looked at her, confusion clouding his gaze, then turned, walked to the fireplace, and braced his arms on the mantelpiece.

Casey took an uncertain breath. She was losing the battle. Matt would not give in. "If I can give up the bonus, why can't you?" she asked, her voice choking at the thought of losing her grandparents' home.

"Casey, you don't know what you're asking. I'm flat broke. I need the money."

She moved to him and placed her hand on his. "Please, Matt. Try to understand. I can't do this. I could never live with myself."

He glanced over at her, then slowly turned to face her. "This really means a lot to you, doesn't it?"

"Yes, it does. Now are you with me on this or not?"

He sighed, bringing his forearms up to rest on her shoulders and dropping his forehead to meet hers. He closed his eyes, as if he were unable to face his next words.

"All right," he breathed. "You win."

Casey stood stock-still, wondering whether she had heard him right. She drew back. Had he actually agreed? She searched his face, but his expression was blank, unreadable. She wanted to believe him, to trust him, but could she?

Without hesitation, she reached up to kiss his lips, and lingered for just a moment longer than was necessary. "Thank you," she whispered. Then she felt inexplicably compelled to kiss him again. "Thank you," she repeated, before her lips met his.

He opened his eyes and looked down at her, desire flooding his gaze. In one smooth motion, he moved his hands to encircle her waist and draw her fully against him. His impatient mouth found hers and she lost herself in the urgency of his kiss. His tongue teased her lips, sending a warm rush of pleasure coursing through her body. His hands glided over her waist and hips, rumpling her damp clothes in an effort to feel the curves and flesh beneath.

Her mind told her to stop, to get him out of the house and away from Ellen's wedding as quickly as possible. But her body's reaction buried her common sense and she gave herself over to the incredible sensations that drove her deeper into his arms.

She reached up to push his jacket from his shoulders and unbutton his shirt. Matt didn't wait for the buttons but interrupted their kiss for a moment while he pulled the shirt off over his head. Then he hungrily found her lips again.

Casey could feel his heart hammering beneath her fingers as she spread her hands over his smooth chest and relished the burning heat of his body. His voice was a caress against her ear as he groaned, "God, Casey. If you don't want this, stop me now."

Her voice was shaky. "I want this. I want you."

His lips skimmed along the curve of her neck and she felt herself losing all control. "And I want you, Casey. I can't make you any promises right now. I wish to God I could, but I can't."

Not *I love you, Casey,* just *I want you.* At least he was being honest. It didn't matter, anyway. She loved him, that's all that really mattered. "It's all right. I don't need promises." Her breath caught as his hands crept under her sweater and spread along her back. "I just need you," she gasped.

He bent his head to look into her eyes as he slowly undressed her, pausing every few seconds to kiss her. With every kiss and every touch, she felt herself becoming bolder and less inhibited, and moments later, she stood before him in her bra and panties, calm and unafraid.

Matt kissed her again as he ran his hands up and down her bare arms, sending shivers along her spine. He took her hands and drew her toward the bed, pulled her down with him into the soft depths of the comforter and covered her with the hard, hot length of him.

She winced slightly as the buttons of his jeans bit into the soft flesh of her stomach. "Garrison, I think you better take these off," she suggested, tugging at the waistband across his back.

His face was buried in the curve of her neck, his tongue tracing an electric path to her ear, and she heard him mumble something unintelligible. When he came up for air several seconds later, he saw the look of pain on her face and his expression fell.

"I'll stop," he said quickly, pulling away. "It's all right."

She smiled, then giggled shyly. He was as nervous as she should have been. Matt Garrison, gorgeously handsome, incredibly worldly, and unbelievably sexy, was nervous about making love to her!

"No. I don't want you to stop. Just take those damn jeans off before the buttons do me in." She rubbed the red marks on her stomach but her fingers were quickly replaced by the brush of his lips.

He pushed himself off the bed, then hastily yanked off his boots and socks and stripped off his jeans and underwear. Her breath caught in her throat as he stood before her, naked, the muscles of his stomach tensed. The light from the window outlined his wide shoulders and narrow hips and the swollen evidence of his desire.

Casey felt the breath leave her body and could barely draw another. Even as he moved away to rummage through his backpack, her eyes remained fixed on him, on his tight buttocks and muscled thighs.

He returned to the bed, his gaze dusky with desire, a tiny smile tugging at his lips. He held up a foil packet then placed it on the bedside table. "I knew that box of pencils would come in handy."

Casey smiled in embarrassment. Birth control. She hadn't thought of that. "Do you always come prepared?" she asked shyly, pushing herself up on one elbow.

He grinned at her, then rolled on top of her and looked down into her eyes. "I bought them in Laramie where I bought your clothes. Right after I decided I was going to make love to you, come hell or high water."

"And what if I had refused you, Garrison?" she said in a teasing voice.

He looked incredulous. "Refuse me? The thought never crossed my mind." She could see he was baiting her and she pushed against his chest with a laugh, then was swept along with him as he rolled over and pulled her on top of him.

"You can have any woman you want," she said, her voice unsteady but needing to hear his answer. "Why me?"

He reached out and ran his finger from her collar-bone to her nipple to flick at the hardened bud. "I don't know. I wish I could figure it out. I've always avoided attachments. One minute I'm there, the next I'm gone. It just goes along with the job, I guess."

"What does?"

"Loneliness."

Casey bent down to kiss him, her long auburn hair creating a curtain around them. "Is that why you need me?" she murmured. "Are you lonely?"

"No," he answered between her feather-light kisses. "I need you because..." He paused for a moment, then took her face in his hands and looked into her eyes. "Because there is something between us, some connection, that I can't explain and I don't understand. I just know I want to make love to you."

"Then quit talking and make love to me, Garrison," she said.

He smiled up at her, running his thumbs along her cheekbones. "Ask me again," he teased. "And this time use my first name. I don't think I've ever heard you call me by my first name."

"Make love to me," she whispered huskily, leaning down to run her tongue along his lower lip. "Matt."

He moaned, then captured her mouth with his. Somewhere in the course of the kiss she found herself divested of her bra and panties. His mouth roamed across her body, setting her senses humming and her mind reeling. His lips, teasing languidly at her nipples, brought each one to a hard bud before he traced a line down her stomach. When his tongue slid along the crevice of her most intimate spot, she thought her heart would stop from the sheer jolt of passion that shook her. He continued his gentle assault until she was mindless with desire. Her hands, clenched in his hair, pushed his head away and at the same time tried to draw him closer.

She didn't even notice when he pulled away to sheathe himself, as she hovered on the brink of an explosive release. Moving above her, he entered her in one strong motion, surging into her slippery warmth. When he had buried himself deep within her, he froze for a moment, his breath coming quickly. Then he began to move slowly and sensuously inside her, his narrow hips rotating against her thighs.

His rhythm increased with each penetration and she tipped her hips up to meet his every thrust. When his hand slid down between their sweat-slicked bodies to touch the center of her desire, she knew she was lost. An explosion of light danced before her eyes and she opened them to see him staring down at her, his eyes clouded with passion. A moan escaped her lips, and at the sound he closed his eyes and threw back his head, his muscles tensed, his movement stilled.

She felt his fulfillment as he arched above her and his shouts of completion echoed through the room. Then he collapsed on top of her and kissed her deeply, the kiss punctuated by his waning shudders and spasms.

Her body tingled, as if millions of tiny pins were pricking her fingers and toes. He felt heavy on top of her, but she loved the feel of his lean, hard body against hers. For a long time, he didn't move and she listened as his ragged breathing began to slow. Tentatively she slid her palms along his back and gently massaged the muscles between his shoulder blades. He sighed, then slowly rolled to his side, and took her with him without breaking their intimate connection.

His eyes were still glazed with passion and he gently touched his mouth to hers, kissing her, tasting her, slowly savoring the aftermath of their lovemaking. "I think I'm falling in love with you, Casey," he whispered. "I don't know what the hell to do about it. I know it can't work, but that doesn't seem to stop how I feel."

Casey looked deep into his eyes, seeing the raw truth of his words reflected in his expression. "And I think I love you, Matt Garrison," she answered, her voice clear and determined. "We don't have to stop it. We can just let it be."

The sound of his soft, even breathing lulled her into a dreamless slumber. It didn't matter what the future held for them, she thought as she drifted off to sleep. At that moment, nothing mattered but the fact that they loved each other. And whether they spent the next fifty years together or apart, nothing would change her feelings for Matt Garrison.

# 8

*When I woke up there were people gathered around me, heatedly discussing how I could have ended up lying unconscious in the middle of a parking garage. It's amazing how the state of public unconsciousness in L.A. automatically makes a person a drunk or a derelict. My muscles screamed in agony as I pulled myself to a sitting position and reached up to feel the growing goose egg on the back of my head. My purse was beside me, but the address book was gone. It didn't take much thought to figure out who had it. He knew sooner or later I'd find it. All he had to do was wait until I did.*

*I don't make many mistakes, but when I do they're big ones. Underestimating him ranked near the top of the list. Trusting him took the prize.*

THE SOUND of running water could be heard through the bathroom door, accompanied by a cheerful but hopelessly out of tune version of "Get Happy." Matt smiled, then closed her notebook. Yesterday she had completed another ten or eleven pages of manuscript. The plot of her novel had become so compelling that his curiosity had gotten the better of him and he had rifled through her belongings for another look. His opinion of her work hadn't changed; she was talented. Not just as a writer, but in other surprising and unexpected ways, he thought to himself.

He stretched sinuously, working his pleasantly exhausted muscles. They had slept for only a few hours at a time since they had tumbled into bed yesterday morning, yet he felt exhilarated, on top of the world. Both lunch and dinner had been eaten in front of the bedroom fireplace, in between their bouts of incredible sex. They hadn't heard a sound from the rest of the house and assumed Ellen and David were similarly occupied.

Casey was more than he had expected. She loved him with a sweet combination of reckless abandon and shy insecurity, an uninhibited enchantress one minute and a bashful schoolgirl the next. She possessed him as nothing and no one had ever done in the past. He felt bewitched by her, hopelessly caught by the magnetism that seemed to surround her.

Matt laughed out loud and shook his head. He was waxing romantic. He, Matt Garrison, last of the world's great cynics. Love was something for workaday fools, an overblown emotion that had only one purpose—to tie two people inescapably together until they grew so bored with life they stopped living and began existing.

Nevertheless he loved Casey Carmichael. He wanted to spend the rest of his life making her happy. The rest of his life . . . making her happy . . .

Matt frowned, sitting down on the edge of the bed at the sudden realization. Could he make her happy? He had nothing to offer her. With a total net worth of around fifty thousand dollars in camera equipment and no regular income, how could he expect to provide for her? He barely made enough money to feed himself. Sure, she had a job with a decent salary and it was the nineties after all. But he wanted to give her her dream, the security to work on her novel full-time.

Matt brought his elbows to his knees, then lowered his head to rest in his hands. For the first time in his adult life, he began to understand the meaning of the word "practical."

*Yes, Garrison, be practical. How do you expect to make a relationship work when the most you have to offer is a satisfying roll in the hay whenever you blow into town?*

And how often would that be? Would Casey be happy with a man who spent the majority of his time out of the country? And would he be happy taking only those jobs that kept him close to home? The impossibility of their relationship began to sink in by degrees. He had nothing to offer her.

Matt Garrison, son of one of the wealthiest men in Boston, a once-upon-a-time heir to an immense banking empire, didn't have two nickels to rub together. Maybe his father had the right idea all along. What difference does love make if you haven't got the money to back it all up?

He could always go back to the family. *The* family. That's how his brother and sister referred to it, as if it had an identity of its own, beyond those of its members. There had been overtures of peace in the past couple of years, but Matt had ignored them. He had kept his distance and communicated only when it suited him. Maybe it was time to put the past in the past. For Casey's sake. For the sake of love.

The sound of running water ceased and he hastily stuffed her notebook back into her tote bag. As he tucked it between the folds of a sweater, he noticed a sheaf of papers hidden near the bottom. He pulled them out and scanned the text. The story he read confused him at first, for he was looking at a story that should have never been put to paper.

He was reading an account of Emily Harrington's wedding.

A nagging suspicion took control of his thoughts. When had she written the story? And what did she intend to do with it? She had been so adamant about getting him to drop the story. Just what kind of game was she playing?

He quickly shoved the folded papers into the back pocket of his jeans and shook the thoughts from his head. All of his instincts rebelled at the thought of her deception. She had probably started the story before she had had a change of heart. He trusted her. She would have an explanation for the story.

Moments later, she stood in the doorway, her slender body wrapped in a towel, her damp hair falling in tangled tendrils to her shoulders.

"Morning," she said, a trace of shyness in her voice.

His doubts dissolved at the sight of her luminous smile. She was quite possibly the most beautiful woman in the world. Not beautiful in the stunning sense of the word, but beautiful in her own serene, unassuming way. Her brilliant green eyes cautiously searched his face as his eyes roamed across her body. He remembered every inch of silken skin, every soft curve now hidden by the folds of the bath towel.

"Morning," he said. He tried to hide his arousal but this was impossible, since he hadn't bothered to get dressed and sat on the bed totally nude.

He stood up and walked across the room, watching her eyes widen at the sight of his nakedness and undisguised reaction to her. Slowly he lowered his head and touched his lips to hers. An immediate shock of sensation ran through his limbs to meet at the hard ridge between his legs.

She pulled away and gazed up at him. "Matt, we really should get going. We have a long drive ahead of—"

"Later," he growled, covering her mouth again.

She wrapped her arms around his neck and her fingers slid through his hair. She stood on tiptoe to probe the depths of his mouth with her tongue, and pressed herself fully against him, her hips cradling his growing erection.

Matt felt himself losing control, his actions driven by an elemental force, sensible thought replaced by sensual demand. His doubts and fears melted away and he felt as if he would drown in his hunger for her. Her towel dropped to the floor and his hands touched her. She was warm and wet and ready for him.

She moaned, then pulled her mouth from his to utter incoherent words of passion as her lips skimmed across his chest. Her broken sentences spurred him on and he had to fight an urge to climax right then and there.

With no effort at all, he picked her up, wrapped her legs around his waist and rested her back against the wall. He probed her mouth with his tongue and his stiff shaft teased the swollen bud of her passion. Common sense told him to stop, to get some protection, but her tiny sobs of pleasure drove him forward. He wanted to touch her without barriers, to become one with her, if only for a moment. Just once, he thought, determined to pull out after one stroke.

But he hadn't counted on the jolt of desire that raced through him as he slowly buried himself inside her. "Don't move," he said through clenched teeth, his words a mixture of harsh command and urgent request. How could he have been so stupid? How could he have ever considered taking such a risk?

"Umm . . ."

He felt her shift slightly and another tremor raced through him.

"Casey, stop. Just stay still. I need to get some protection."

She moaned and he felt her breath against his ear. "No," she whispered. "I don't want anything between us. I just want you."

"But what if . . ."

"It's all right," she said, tugging gently at his hair and pulling his head back. Her lips were puffy from his kisses and her eyes were cloudy with raw longing. "Trust me," she said with a smile. Her tongue traced across the crease of his mouth. "Trust me."

With a groan, he withdrew, then denying his common sense, he plunged into her again and again.

If the result of their temporary lapse in judgment resulted in a child, that was all the better. It would tie them together permanently, irrevocably; no matter what the future held, he would always be a part of her life. His love for her coursed through his veins and warmed his every breath. She belonged to him, now and forever.

He felt her muscles contract around him and he knew her release was near. He drove into her, feeling his own climax building, reaching beyond the point of return. Grasping each other until they were as close as they could possibly be, they met their pinnacle together in one earthshaking explosion.

Somehow, they ended up on the bed, wrapped in each other's arms, legs tangled together. Matt enjoyed the feel of her cheek against his neck, the butterfly touch of her eyelashes, and for a long time he did not move. Then he looked at his watch. It was 9:00 a.m.

"Sweetheart, are you awake?"

Casey didn't respond, her breathing deep and even.

A soft knock sounded on the door and Matt carefully extracted himself from her embrace. He pulled on his jeans, padded to the door and opened it a crack. Ellen stood in the hallway, a bright smile on her face.

"Good morning," she said cheerfully. "Is Casey awake?"

Matt shook his head. "She's still asleep."

"I'm so glad Casey talked you into staying," Ellen whispered. "I just wanted to let you know that the wedding is set for ten."

Her words hit Matt like an iron fist in the gut. "The wedding?"

"Yes. You and Casey are going to be our witnesses, didn't she tell you? As soon as she wakes up, tell her to come to my room. I have a dress for her to wear."

"Sure," Matt answered, his voice as tight as the knot in his stomach. "I'll tell her." He quietly closed the door and turned to the bed.

In one swift instant his trust in her disappeared. How long had she known about the wedding? And why had she decided to keep it from him? She slept on, an innocent smile curving the corners of her luscious mouth. He sat down on the bed and reached over to run his finger down her bare arm. She stirred, then opened her eyes and looked at him drowsily.

"What time is it?" she asked.

"It's late."

"How late?"

"Too late." His voice was cold, emotionless. "Ellen is up. She came by. She's anxious to talk to you."

She pushed herself up in bed and looked at him hesitantly.

"Is something wrong, Carmichael?"

"No. Nothing. I just forgot to tell you . . ." Her voice drifted off.

"Forgot to tell me what?"

"We have to stay just a little longer. I, um, I promised Ellen that we would serve as witnesses . . . at their marriage ceremony."

"Their marriage ceremony? Why didn't you tell me about this earlier?" he said, his voice icy, yet calm.

"I don't know," she answered defensively. "What difference does it make? We decided to drop the story, didn't we? It doesn't matter."

Matt stood up and shouted, "It doesn't matter? I'm supposed to believe that?"

"Yes. It's the truth."

Running his fingers through his hair, he turned to look at her. She didn't trust him. After all they had shared the night before, after his admission of love, she still didn't trust him. He remembered her promise to him at the airport. No more lies, isn't that what she had said?

He had just caught her in one lie. He remembered the story in his back pocket. He pulled out the papers, unfolded them and threw them on the bed.

"Would you like to explain this?" he said.

"Where did you get those?" she cried.

"Never mind where I got it. Just explain it."

"I wrote that earlier. Before I decided to drop the story. You have to believe that."

"Why didn't you tell me about the wedding?"

"I was planning to. I just didn't know—"

"Whether to trust me?"

"No! I mean, yes. I—I don't know!" she shouted, her voice crackling with emotion. "Maybe I didn't trust you then. But I trust you now. You made a promise to me and I know you'll keep it." She looked at him, her eyes wide and unhappy.

He grabbed his shirt from the floor and pulled it on. "And what was last night? Did you feel the need for a little added insurance?"

Casey jumped out of bed and stormed up to him, her hair flying wildly about her face. She stood nose to chin with him and pushed her finger into his bare chest. "Don't you dare try to turn last night into some kind of manipulation. I meant what I said." She looked glorious, her naked body still rosy and flushed from their lovemaking and he felt a familiar tightening in his groin.

"Did you, Casey?" He paused to button his shirt, deliberately turning away from her. "I wish I could believe that." He grabbed his boots and socks, stalked to the door, yanked it open then turned to face her. "Get your things packed. The minute the ceremony is over, you and I are out of here."

Matt closed the door firmly behind him, resisting the urge to slam it. When he reached the end of the hall he stopped, then turned around to make his way back to the room. Halfway back down the hall he turned again and, with a growl of frustration, slammed his fist into the rough-hewn planks that paneled the walls.

Damn! What the hell had happened? How had such an incredible morning turned into such a disaster? God, the woman had an uncanny way of making him crazy. Crazy with lust, crazy with anger and confusion, just plain crazy.

He paused to bring his rage under control. Calm down, think about this, his mind advised. Maybe she didn't deserve his anger. Maybe she had just forgotten to tell him. Or maybe she was afraid to tell him after what they'd shared. He wanted to believe her. His heart told him she was telling the truth, but his mind knew better.

The master of manipulation had been outdone by a mere amateur. She was lying.

As he tried to sort out his feelings, he realized that he wasn't nearly as angry at her as he was at himself. In the past, he had always been able to maintain a safe distance in his relationships with women. It had served as a buffer against the trouble that a romantic commitment could cause. It had helped to make leaving easier. But his defenses had quickly crumbled in Casey's presence and he realized that he had made himself totally vulnerable.

If this was what love did to a person, he wanted no part of it. He felt stupid, weak, blind. He was a fool to believe that their relationship could work. There was too much standing between them. Her mistrust of him. His mistrust of her. His inability to support her.

He had always lived by the axiom that money couldn't buy happiness. Matt wondered if he had been fooling himself all these years. Maybe his father had it right all along. Love was transitory. Money was the only thing that lasted. And in the end, it all came down to the money.

Exactly twenty-five thousand dollars stood between them. And the same amount would destroy them.

BY THE TIME Ellen knocked on the bedroom door a half hour later, Casey had her angry tears under control.

She watched through red-rimmed eyes as Ellen whisked into the room, a garment bag over her shoulder. Ellen was dressed in a simple yet sophisticated ivory ballerina-length gown. "You look lovely," Casey sighed.

Ellen smiled radiantly. "I feel beautiful." She laid the garment bag on the bed and unzipped it. Inside was a stunning emerald green satin dress. "I found this in the closet," she whispered. "J. D. Latimer, the producer of my last movie, owns this house. J.D.'s wife, Chantalle, has impeccable and very expensive taste in clothing. She's French and she's just about your size. I'm sure she wouldn't mind if you wore it."

Casey examined the dress and noted the name of an exclusive Beverly Hills designer stitched in the tag at the neckline. "It's lovely, but I couldn't," she said, although she was already imagining what she would look like and how Matt would react to her in the dress. She hadn't worn a party dress in ages and she'd never worn one as alluring as the gown that lay before her.

Ellen pushed the dress into her arms and drew her toward the bathroom. "Of course you can. You have to look nice. David found Matt a jacket and tie to wear, so you need to dress up, too. And Matt volunteered to take pictures. He's so sweet. David and I never thought of pictures. At least our families will get to see the wedding photos."

Casey turned back to Ellen, not believing what she had just heard, but Ellen was already at the bedroom door. "There are matching shoes in the garment bag along with a new pair of panty hose. If the shoes don't fit, just come in your stocking feet. We'll have Matt cut all the photos off below the knees." Ellen giggled, then waved as she rushed out the door. "I'll be back in fifteen minutes," she called from the hallway.

Fifteen minutes later, Casey stood before the full-length bathroom mirror, frantically trying to bring some semblance of order to her unruly hair. It had been wet when she stepped out of the shower earlier that morning, but over the course of the following hour's "activities" it had dried into a wild mass of waves and curls.

The dress seemed to lend an air of sexy sophistication to her untamed hair and she decided to leave it unbound, allowing it to fall naturally around her face. The off-the-shoulder shawl collar of the dress displayed a creamy expanse of neck and chest. It fitted tightly around her rib cage and waist, then flared into a wide, crinolined skirt that ended just above her knees. It was a party dress, made for dancing and flirting.

The shoes were stiff and new and a size too big, but Casey slipped her feet inside them, then twirled in front of the mirror. She stopped to stare at herself and noticed the creases of worry on her forehead.

Questions about Matt had been nagging at her mind since Ellen had walked out. He had volunteered to photograph the wedding. She wanted to trust him, wanted to believe that he would keep his promise to her, but she wasn't sure. After their fight this morning, he might decide to back out of his promise and go ahead with the story.

What was he up to? She would have to keep a close eye on him. She wasn't about to let him ruin Ellen and David's wedding day.

Casey heard the door to the bedroom open and her heart skipped a beat. Wondering if Matt had returned, she stepped out of the bathroom ready to demand an explanation from him, but came face-to-face with Ellen. Behind her, the ranch foreman, Hank Willis, stood uncomfortably, tugging on the collar of his shirt and fiddling with the bola tie at his neck.

"I knew that dress would look marvelous on you," Ellen cried. "Hank, doesn't she look beautiful?"

Hank uttered a polite "Yes, ma'am," then tugged at his tie again.

"Hank is going to give the bride away," Ellen explained. "Are you ready?"

Casey nodded and the three of them moved into the hallway. The sounds of Bach drifted back from the living room. Ellen kissed Casey on the cheek, then handed her a bundle of silk flowers that Casey recognized as half of an arrangement that had once decorated the library. Ellen clutched the other half in her hand.

Casey began a slow march through the hallway and into the living room, Ellen and Hank close behind her. The justice of the peace stood in front of the huge fireplace, David and Matt on his left. Although the morning sunshine spilled in through the windows, lighted candles lining the mantelpiece gave the room a romantic ambiance.

Casey's eyes were drawn immediately to Matt, who looked back at her through the lens of his camera. He lowered the camera slowly as she approached, his eyes fixed on her. The dress had done the trick, she thought to herself, smiling inwardly at the hypnotized look on Matt Garrison's face.

She watched as he dragged himself out of his trance and brought the camera up to focus first on her, then on Ellen and Hank. The sound of the automatic winder blended with the soft strains of the Bach suite. As he lowered the camera for a second time, she shot him a suspicious look which he returned with a sardonic smile.

*Just what are you up to, Garrison?* she wondered as she watched him move into a better position to capture the bride and groom on film.

The wedding ceremony passed in a blur. Casey kept one uneasy eye on Matt and the other on the bride and groom. Matt moved silently around the assembled participants, snapping pictures, then quickly returning to perform his duties as best man. Oddly, she found herself the subject of Matt's photography as often as the bride and the groom were.

Ellen and David were oblivious to Matt's activities, so enraptured with each other that they barely blinked when his flash went off. After only ten minutes, they were pronounced husband and wife to the accompaniment of joyous laughter.

Casey watched as Matt began to rewind a roll of film, her heart hammering, wondering if her suspicions would be confirmed. She kept her eyes fixed on the film and a rush of relief coursed through her as Matt handed it to David. He had kept his promise. His offer to serve as wedding photographer was simply a generous gesture and not motivated by the twenty-five-thousand-dollar bonus. She felt guilty. It had been a mistake not to trust him.

An impromptu wedding reception got into full swing when David put some soft music on the stereo system and gallantly asked his new bride to dance. Food was the only thing missing from the reception and Casey decided to raid the kitchen. She discovered a bottle of champagne in the back of the refrigerator. Cheese and crackers would make do for hors d'oeuvres.

"It's not nice for the bridesmaid to be more beautiful than the bride." She turned to find Matt standing in the kitchen doorway, his hip against the doorjamb, much as he had that first night in her apartment. Only this time his teasing attitude was gone, replaced by a manner that was distant and reserved.

Casey turned away from him, feeling her defenses rise. "In all the excitement, Ellen forgot about food."

Matt came up behind her and stood as close as he could without touching her.

Casey sensed his proximity was more of a challenge than an affectionate gesture and she groped for something to say. "I-it was very nice of you to volunteer to take photos of the wedding. It means a lot to Ellen and David."

He placed his hands on either side of her and trapped her between the counter and his body. With a ragged breath, she turned to face him and reached hesitantly to brush an imaginary speck of lint from the lapel of his jacket, her eyes avoiding his cold gaze.

"I'm sorry about this morning," she began. "I didn't mean to keep it from you. I just wasn't sure you'd agree to drop the story. I should have told you about the wedding when I learned about it. I was wrong not to trust you." She waited for him to reciprocate, to offer his own apologies for his part in their argument. When he didn't, she risked a glance up at him.

His face was entirely unreadable. He dropped his hands to his sides then shrugged his shoulders. "Then again, maybe you were right," he said and turned and walked out of the kitchen.

Casey opened her mouth to call out to him, but stopped herself. She angrily picked up a box of crackers and ripped open the top. All right! She had made a mistake. She should have trusted him, but considering all that had happened in the past few days, didn't she have a right to doubt him just a little? Their relationship had begun with distrust and deception. After last night, she had hoped they would have been beyond that.

Lord, Matt Garrison could be stubborn. She had offered an apology, hadn't she? He didn't have to hold a grudge over such a petty argument. If he expected their relationship to work, he would have to learn to kiss and make up.

Casey quickly finished arranging the cheese and crackers, then placed the plate, the champagne and six glasses on a tray and headed back to the living room, determined to persuade Matt to forgive her. After all, they loved each other, didn't they?

Some inner voice told Casey to slow down as she approached the living room and she stood in the shadows of the hallway and gathered her resolve. Matt was standing near the end table, sorting through his camera equipment while Ellen and David danced. Hank had disappeared and the justice of the peace, Mr. McCoy, sat snoozing in an overstuffed armchair.

Casey's eyes roamed over Matt's long, lean frame and she admired the way he looked in a jacket and tie. Though he still wore his blue jeans, the jacket changed his whole appearance, made him look more stable and settled. His brow was furrowed in concentration as he worked. He stopped only long enough to glance over his shoulder at Ellen and David.

Casey marveled at the strength of his hands and the dexterity of his long, slender fingers, and remembered how, just hours ago, they had driven her over the brink of passion. His movements were assured, competent, as if he knew his camera by heart. Maybe someday he would know her body by heart. He would know every pleasure point, every nerve ending.

Then, very slowly, the significance of his actions dawned on her and she watched in growing disbelief as he removed an exposed roll of film from his camera and quickly placed it in the front pocket of his camera bag. His movements were calm and precise as he loaded another roll into the camera, rewound it immediately, popped it back out and placed it on the mantelpiece next to one other roll.

Casey stepped back, away from the sight of Matt's betrayal. She felt her heart constrict painfully and realized she had been holding her breath as she watched him. Her head was spinning and her pulse was racing and she stumbled slightly as she leaned back against the wall. The champagne glasses clinked together softly, but she quickly recovered her senses and stilled her shaky hands.

No! It couldn't be! How could he do this after he had promised to drop the story? She had allowed herself to trust him so completely that she had given her heart and body. And when she hadn't told him about the wedding, he had accused *her* of using sex to manipulate *him*. How clever to turn the tables on her like that, when all along he was the one who was doing the manipulating. She had been taken in by him, thoroughly and stupidly seduced by a master.

And she had fallen in love. With an honorable man, a man capable of love and a man worthy of trust. With a man who never existed. All he cared about was the money—twenty-five thousand dollars. Not half of it, but all of it. She doubted that he had ever intended to split it with her.

*Damn you, Matt Garrison! You're not going to get away with this. Not if I have anything to say about it.*

She stepped into the living room with a smile on her face. "I think it's time to toast the bride and groom," she said with forced gaiety. She placed the tray on a table, poured the champagne and passed around the glasses. The justice of the peace continued to sleep.

When the four of them had gathered in the center of the room, Casey cleared her throat and raised her glass. "To Ellen and David," she began. "To the love you share. And to trust and honesty and joy and comfort. May your marriage be filled with all the very best that life and love have to offer."

Matt looked over at her and silently raised his glass to her before putting it to his lips. She forced a smile, then turned to Ellen and David. "And now, I think that Matt and I are going to say goodbye and let you two start your honeymoon."

Ellen smiled sadly. "The honeymoon's only going to last one day. David has a trial and I've got to get back to California."

"Then you two had better get started." Casey stepped over to Ellen and gave her a hug. "Thank you for everything," she whispered. Ellen's eyes began to mist and she smiled at Casey in return, unable to speak. Casey turned to David and squeezed his outstretched hand. "Take good care of her."

"I will," David answered. "If you two are ever in New York, please look us up." He reached into the breast pocket of his suit and pulled out a silver case, extracted a plain white business card and handed it to Casey.

"Wait." Ellen snatched the card from Casey's fingers and grabbed a pen from the desk, then scribbled something on the card. "This is my phone number in L.A. Call me. Just to talk."

"Thank you," Casey mumbled, her voice cracking slightly. She wondered whether the invitation would stand in another month. Could she stop Matt from turning in the story? She sure as hell was going to try.

Matt shook hands with David then kissed Ellen on the cheek. They made their way back to the bedroom to gather their belongings and to change. Both were silent as they packed and left the ranch house.

CASEY STARED OUT the window as Matt swung the truck off I-25 and onto the ramp for I-70. The freeway sign indicated that the exit for Stapleton International was only four miles farther. Her back was turned to him as she lay curled up in her seat, feigning sleep, but she could sense his eyes on her. Her body felt stiff and her legs were cramped from maintaining the same position for nearly three hours. She had "fallen asleep" shortly after they'd left the ranch house and the ruse had effectively killed any conversation between them. It had also given her time to think.

Matt pulled the truck to a halt in the rental car parking lot. Casey tensed slightly when he gently shook her awake, then she turned and forced a yawn.

"Are we there already?" she asked as she stretched the kinks out of her body. She glanced at Matt, then took a closer look. His face looked drawn; dark shadows smudged the skin beneath his eyes and his mouth was set in a grim line.

He reached out to caress her cheek, but Casey pulled back. She chided herself inwardly for her mistake, then made up for it by smiling warmly at him.

"Casey, we need to talk," Matt said, his voice uncertain.

Casey hopped out of the truck and walked to the back for her bags. "We can talk on the plane," she said, trying to cover her nervousness. She pulled Matt's camera bag from the truck and felt her fingers grow numb. She was so close. Then he grabbed the bag from her and she let it go reluctantly. Be patient, she said to herself.

They walked into the airport and made their way to the rental-car counter. Casey's eyes darted between Matt and his camera bag as he paid for the truck.

From there they went to the ticket counter. Casey felt her pulse begin to quicken. Would it work? She wouldn't know until she tried.

Casey stopped suddenly. "I don't feel very well."

Matt turned to look at her, a frown of concern on his face.

"I think I'd better sit down." Casey slowly made her way to a bench, dropped her bags and sat carefully down. She raised her hand to her forehead for effect and closed her eyes for dramatic emphasis.

Matt sat down beside her, took her icy hand and rubbed it between his. "What's wrong? Are you afraid of flying again?"

Casey gritted her teeth. He almost sounded genuinely concerned. She shot him a mournful look, then sighed. "No, I don't think that's it. I feel a little dizzy. Maybe I'm just hungry. I haven't eaten all day and then that glass of champagne..." Casey took a deep breath, waiting patiently before she dangled the bait and set the hook. "Could you—"

"You wait here while I go find you something to eat," Matt offered, giving her hand a pat. "Then I'll take care of our tickets." Matt stood and looked down at her. "Stay put," he said, his voice warm and rich. "I'll be back in a second." His face brightened when she returned his smile and she watched as he strode away.

When he was finally out of sight, Casey reached down, opened the front pocket of his camera bag and withdrew the roll of exposed film. She stowed the film carefully in her jacket pocket, then picked up her bags and quickly walked toward the sliding glass doors that led out of the terminal. She hopped into the first available taxi, sat back and slowly let out her breath.

"Take me to the bus terminal," she said to the taxi driver. "Checkmate," she said to herself as the taxi pulled away.

# 9

The lock on the front door took a minute and a half. The house was dark when I entered, but I knew the floor plan well. I was in the library no more than ten seconds when the room was suddenly flooded with light. I spun around to see him standing in the door. "Theo," he said, casually rubbing his cheek with the barrel of his .357 Magnum. "I've been expecting you. I suppose you've come for the book?" He came closer, still fondling the gun a little too intimately for my taste. Then he held out the book to me. I took it, shocked at how easily he gave it up. He must have read my expression. "There's a page missing," he explained, his voice coldly seductive. "The one with my name on it."

"You'll never change, will you?" I asked. It was a stupid question. And I knew the answer before I asked it. A man's gotta be what a man's gotta be. He'd told me that once before. I guess I had just chosen to forget it.

A GRAY AND HAZY daylight was breaking over Las Vegas as the Greyhound bus pulled into the terminal. The neon lights of the casinos, visible from the interstate, blinked their garish twenty-four-hour-a-day welcome.

Casey sat near the front, her notebook spread across her lap, her mood as gray as the sky. A fleeting memory of her childhood trip to Las Vegas called forth a dim vision of Louise, bleached blond hair and red fingernails, and she smiled.

She glanced down at her watch, and calculated her arrival time in Los Angeles. She had caught the 3:00 p.m. bus out of Denver. After a late dinner stop at a greasy spoon in Grand Junction, she had fallen asleep minutes after the bus had pulled out of the restaurant parking lot. The combination of jangling emotions and sheer exhaustion had made the long ride through Utah a blank.

It would be another seven hours before the bus rolled into Los Angeles. She would arrive at 12:30 p.m., Tuesday afternoon, exactly a week to the very hour after she had met Matt Garrison in the hotel closet of the Beverly Palms.

How could her life have changed so much in such a short time? In less than a week she had fallen in and out of love. When she had thought about falling in love in the past, she had always imagined love as a long, leisurely walk toward a flower-bedecked altar rather than a headlong race off the edge of a cliff.

Before she met Matt Garrison her life had been well-ordered, quiet, and sometimes, she admitted to herself, a little boring. Loving Matt Garrison had been the most exhilarating time of her entire life. And witnessing his betrayal had been the most painful.

Casey reached into her jacket pocket and pulled out the roll of film. Everything they had shared, everything they had meant to each other had been wiped away by a roll of Kodak Ektachrome film. Was it worth it? Had Matt thought so little of what they had shared that he was willing to destroy it all for money?

A lump filled her throat and she fought back tears. Matt had never really cared for her. All he cared about was the bonus. Not his share of the bonus, but the entire bonus. She had no doubt that Matt's photos of Ellen and David's wedding would have been splashed across the cover of the next issue of *The Inquisitor* and he would have walked away twenty-five-thousand-dollars richer because of them.

She had been sorely tempted to throw the film away, but she decided to keep it as evidence of his perfidy. When she got back to L.A., she would send it to David and Ellen, with some excuse about the roll getting mixed up in Matt's belongings. That would put an end to the entire episode. He could still file a story, but so could she. And she would fill hers with so many outrageous lies that Art Griswold would prefer her version of the "truth" to the real version.

Casey stepped into the aisle of the bus, her stomach grumbling with hunger. A 6:00 a.m. breakfast in Las Vegas wasn't much to look forward to. But her thoughts were not on Las Vegas, they were focused on Los Angeles seven hours down the road.

She would stop Matt Garrison, no matter what it took.

THE INTERIOR OF THE Los Angeles bus terminal was hot and stuffy. The voice on the crackling intercom had announced the arrival of the 12:15 bus from San Francisco three minutes earlier. The Denver bus was due in another fifteen minutes. Matt stood near the door and watched as the passengers walked through and greeted family and friends who had come to meet them. As the flow of passengers dwindled, he turned and resumed his restless pacing.

How would she react? Would she smile? Or would her face show surprise and distaste at his presence? A gambling man would no doubt place money on a face filled with anger and maybe even a little scorn.

He had returned to the bench at the Denver airport to find his camera bag and backpack lying on the floor, abandoned. At first, he was annoyed that she had left his equipment unattended and he glanced around, certain she would be close by. When he couldn't find her, a wave of panic overtook him and wild visions of kidnapping raced through his mind. Like a fool, he had walked up and down the concourse for nearly twenty minutes looking for her, asking airport personnel whether they had seen her. He wondered if she had fallen ill and been helped away to find medical assistance. It wasn't until he sat down on the bench where he had originally left her that he had noticed the open front pocket of his camera bag.

In an explosive rush, the pieces had fallen into place. She had never intended to get on a plane with him that afternoon. Considering her paralyzing fear of flying, she had been quite calm as they entered the airport. Too calm, as if her mind had been occupied with something else. And then there was her sudden illness. It hadn't taken much effort to get rid of him, just a little swoon and a sweetly feminine smile.

Somehow she had found out about the film. The only
way she could have known for certain was if she had
seen him take the film from the camera and put it into
his bag. She must have been watching from the hallway. His mind flashed back to her distant behavior and
forced laughter when she had returned from the
kitchen.

She obviously hadn't seen him remove it from his bag
and put it into his jacket pocket, though. Wouldn't Art
Griswold be surprised when Casey Carmichael handed
him the Hollywood wedding of the year complete with
pictures of mule deer in their winter habitat?

It served her right. He had grossly underestimated
Casey Carmichael's desire for the twenty-five-
thousand-dollar bonus. She had never intended to
share it with him; she planned on turning in *her* story
and *his* photos on her own. And she had almost gotten
away with it. She had nearly convinced him to drop the
story, going so far as to use seduction to insure his
compliance with her plan.

How ironic that he had taken the pictures to give to
her. He had wanted her to have her dream; it was the
only thing he could possibly give her that was worth
anything. When she had acted guilty about intruding
on Ellen's wedding, he had assumed that sooner or later
she would regret her decision to drop the story and regret her decision to give up her dream. And he would
have been there to hand it back to her.

Until she decided to steal it for herself.

Matt shook his head in self-disgust. He had never
been a gullible man. He had never been a lot of things
until he met Casey. But then she had blown into his life

and changed it forever. Freedom would never feel the same again; there would always be a part of him that longed for the feeling of total contentment that he had experienced for a brief time with Casey Carmichael. Now, he would always know that there was something missing, that what he had was no longer perfect but flawed by her absence and ruined by her deception.

Matt turned to watch another busload of passengers enter the terminal. Ten more minutes. Ten more minutes until he could settle things once and for all with Casey Carmichael.

CASEY SAW HIM as soon as she walked inside the terminal. His piercing blue eyes scanned the crowd and she knew immediately she was the target of his search. She turned her shoulder to him, lowered her head and sidled alongside an immense man with a tattoo of an eagle on his right forearm and a gold ring in his ear. Her nerves were humming and she reacted with her usual clumsiness in times of stress. In her haste to make it past Garrison, her bag slipped from her hand and fell at the big man's feet. He tripped, falling flat on his face, his legs tangled around her bag.

"Damn it, lady," he growled from his position on the floor, "what the hell are you doing?"

Casey knelt down, absently brushed a crushed cigarette butt from the sleeve of his black Harley-Davidson T-shirt and tugged at her bag, buried under his bulk. "I'm so sorry. Please excuse me. Here, let me help you up." Casey offered him her hand, but the moment he grasped it a lady bumped into Casey from behind and they both fell on top of the man.

The contents of the woman's three shopping bags spilled around them and scattered across the grimy floor. The cloying smell of dime-store perfume mixed with the overpowering stench of stale beer made Casey nauseous as she lay sandwiched between two denizens of Los Angeles bus-station society.

A strong hand hauled her up and she stood face-to-face with the man she had so valiantly tried to avoid. His blue eyes were narrowed, his sensual mouth set in a grim line.

"Lurleen, darlin'," he crooned, his voice like acid. "Welcome home."

He grabbed her bag from the midst of the melee and pulled her alongside him, effectively extracting her from a situation that was becoming more and more ridiculous. Two more people had stumbled on the wreckage of the three-person pileup and the air was filled with colorful curses and high-pitched screeching.

In moments, they were outside the bus terminal. Casey drew in breath of fresh air, then choked on the combination of smog and diesel exhaust fumes from a bus that sat idling at the curb. She looked at Matt through watery eyes. His fingers were clamped around her wrist as he pulled her toward a waiting cab.

Casey yanked her arm from his grasp, then hurried up the sidewalk. Running with her bags was impossible, and for a moment she considered dropping them in an effort to escape. But seconds later, she realized that bags or no bags, Matt was not about to let her get away.

"Let go of me," she snapped, trying to pull from his grasp again. "If you don't let go, I'll scream."

"Go ahead," he said. "Scream your fool head off. It's not going to make any difference. You're still coming with me." He pushed her into a waiting cab then climbed in after her.

"Take me to the nearest police station," Casey ordered the driver as she slid to the far side of the seat and put her bags between them as a wall of defense. "This man is kidnapping me."

"Thirteen seventy-five North Sycamore in West Hollywood," Matt told the driver. The driver looked at her then at Matt, deciding whether to take his orders from the calm male half of the fare or the hysterical female half.

"Look at me," Casey shouted. "I asked you to take me to the nearest police station. Now do it!"

"West Hollywood," Matt repeated. The words were barely out of Matt's mouth before the driver stamped the accelerator and swerved into traffic. The speed threw Casey back against the seat and sent a fringe of plastic beads hanging above the windshield swaying wildly back and forth.

The cab ride was silent. Matt stared straight ahead during their frenzied trip through the streets of downtown L.A. Casey gripped the door handle with a white-knuckled hand, ready to bolt if the perilous cab ride became too much to tolerate.

They were only blocks from her apartment when Matt finally spoke.

"Where's the film, Casey?" His voice held a hint of menace.

Casey looked out the window of the cab at the familiar scenery rushing by. "I don't know what you mean. What film?"

"You know exactly what I'm talking about. Now hand it over."

Casey turned to face him, tense with anger. "You promised me, Garrison. You promised to drop the story and you didn't. I don't have the film. I threw it away."

Matt laughed cynically. "Don't give me that. I may have been stupid enough to believe you once, but I won't make that mistake a second time. You're planning on turning the story in to Griswold. Why would you throw the film away?"

"What?" Casey's anger dissolved into disbelief.

"That sweet innocent act of yours actually had me fooled for a while. You never intended to share the bonus with me."

"What the hell are you talking about?"

"Drop the act, Casey. That's what the whole thing was all the time, wasn't it? An act. I underestimated your abilities, although I have to admire the way you carried it all out. You didn't want me around from the start, but then I surprised you on the plane and you were stuck with me. But you turned it all in your favor at the end. You got the story, you got the photos, and you almost got rid of me."

"How did you know where to find me?"

"You and I both know that you hate to fly, so that left only three ways to get out of Denver and back to Los Angeles. The train and the bus were the next logical choices. Now, if you had rented a car, you might have lost me, but considering your need to get back as quickly as possible, I didn't think you'd bother with the drive. The train for L.A. leaves Denver in the morning, so you would have had to wait an extra day. The bus, however, makes three trips a day to L.A. If you hadn't arrived on one of the buses today, I was prepared to sit at the Amtrak station and wait for you tomorrow."

"Brilliant," Casey muttered sarcastically. "You think you have it all figured out, don't you?"

"Believe me, once I figured out what you were really after, it wasn't too hard to put the rest of the pieces together. It was a very ingenious plan."

"You have a lot of nerve accusing me of exactly what you've been planning all along. You think that if you turn this around on me, it will give you some kind of advantage, don't you? *You're* the one who took the photos after you agreed to drop the story. *You're* the one who planned on turning in the story on your own. And you almost pulled it off, too. If I hadn't seen you put the film in your camera bag, I'd have never known. Not until I saw the pictures plastered all over the front page of *The Inquisitor*. But by then, you would have been safely out of the country with your twenty-five thousand dollars. Don't you dare accuse *me* of being ingenious!"

Matt sat back and crossed his arms over his chest. "Well now, I believe we've reached an impasse. I don't believe you and you don't believe me. The story of our relationship. The fact remains that you still have the film and I want it."

"I don't have it. I told you I threw it away."

"Why would you throw it a—"

"I wasn't planning on turning it in, you blockhead."

"I've heard this story before. And it didn't impress me the first time."

"Well, believe it now, buster. Because it's the truth." The cab came to a screeching halt in front of Casey's apartment building and she hopped out, dragging her bags with her. She was almost at the front door before Matt caught up to her.

"Carmichael, I want that film."

Casey threw down her bags and spun around angrily, her eyes spitting fire. "You want the film? All right, you've got it."

Casey pulled the roll of film out of her pocket and held it up for him to see. He reached out to grab it, but she pulled it away and dropped it in front of her on the concrete sidewalk. As Matt bent to pick it up, she brought the heel of her shoe down on top of it. The two ends of the casing popped off. Casey snatched the broken casing from the ground and yanked the length of film from the spool, exposing the photos on it to the bright California sun.

With a flourish, she took the shiny brown ribbon of exposed film and wrapped it around Matt's neck. "There's your precious film, Garrison. I hope it was worth it." Her voice cracked and she struggled to control her emotions. "I never intended to turn in the story. That's the truth. I took the film because I thought you were going to break your promise." Her voice was a quivering whisper. "I trusted you. I was a fool." She turned to open the front door of her apartment building when Matt's hand grabbed hers.

Casey felt a hot rush of desire as the warm strength of his fingers seeped into her hand. After all he had done, she still thrilled to his touch. Maybe her body would betray her, but she wouldn't allow her mind the same freedom. She pushed the door open with her shoulder, anxious to shut it behind her, to close the door on Matt Garrison and everything they had shared.

"Casey, wait." His voice was soft and subdued; the sarcasm and disgust were gone.

"Let me go, Garrison. You got what you came for, now leave."

He turned her around to face him. Rather than fight him, she let her muscles relax. She was tired of fighting, bone tired. She just wanted to crawl into bed and shut out the world and everything in it for the next three years. Why couldn't he let her go? Hadn't they said everything there was to be said?

He gently reached under her chin and tipped her face up to meet his gaze. But instead of seeing anger in his eyes, she saw regret. She studied his face, trying to understand his odd turnabout. What was he after now? The film was gone. What else could he possibly want from her?

"You're not the fool, Casey, I am. I'm sorry," he said, his voice husky with emotion. "I made a mistake."

"It's too late for apologies, Garrison. I don't want to hear your excuses."

"I'm not giving you excuses, I'm just trying to explain. I'm sorry I didn't believe you. Somehow, I knew you didn't double-cross me; deep down inside, I knew. But the road between my heart and my brain isn't traveled very often. I just got sidetracked." She saw a sheepish smile break across his face and she once again was struck by how incredibly handsome he was.

"That doesn't change the fact that you took those photos after you promised me you'd drop the story."

"I know I promised to drop the story and I did. I didn't take the pictures for me, I took them for you, Casey."

Casey looked at him in shocked incredulity. With a disgusted laugh, she turned to the door. But he brought her around again and pulled her close against his chest. She pushed against him, wriggling out of his embrace.

"Don't insult me, Garrison. I may be naive, but I'm not stupid."

"I wanted you to have your dream, Casey." Her name sounded like a caress on his lips. "It was the only way I could give it to you. I have nothing to offer you. Your father, wherever he may be, would call me a man without prospects. I just wanted you to have your dream."

"You don't know anything about my dream," Casey said, her eyes filling with tears. "You don't know anything about me. We're complete strangers, Garrison. We've built a relationship on lies and deceptions. Like a house of cards, it was all bound to come tumbling down sooner or later."

He drew her against his chest and smoothed her hair with his hands. "I know, I know. But we can start again, Casey. We can put this all behind us and start over."

Casey sniffled and reached up to wipe the tears away with her fingers. "Come on, Garrison. Let's be honest here. You and I are like fire and water. We'd end up destroying each other. Why don't we just chalk the whole thing up to experience and go on with our lives?"

He pushed her away from him and looked into her face, his eyes probing hers. "Is that what you want?"

Casey took a ragged breath. "Yes," she lied. "That's what I want."

"Well, it's not what I want!"

"You can't always have everything you want, Garrison. You'll recover."

"I want to marry you, Casey."

She looked at him in utter shock. "You want to marry me? Why?"

Matt shrugged his shoulders and smiled. "Damned if I know. Maybe because I think I'm in love with you. And because I'm pretty sure you're in love with me. All I know is that I want you here when I get back, and if marriage is the only way to insure that, then that's what I want."

"Such a charming proposal. What sensible girl could refuse?" She laughed caustically. "No, Garrison. I won't marry you. Not now, not ever."

"You will marry me, Casey. I can promise you that. I'm not going to let this go. You and I are going to work this out as soon as I get back."

"Get back?" Casey asked.

Matt's eyes filled with pride and excitement and he watched her face intently. "I stopped by my buddy's house last night to collect my messages. There was a message there from the photo editor at *World Geographic*. He wants me for a photo essay on rural China. I was supposed to leave yesterday." He shook his head and laughed. "Can you believe it? I took the film so I would have something to give you, and all the time I had it all. It was waiting for me right here in L.A. The job pays big bucks and it's a terrific break. It's big league, Casey."

"How long are you going to be gone?"

"Two months, maybe three at the most."

Casey sighed. "Congratulations, Garrison. I know how much this means to you."

"How much it means to us," he said as he lowered his lips to hers. His kiss was brief, but incredibly sweet. "This will give us a start, a solid beginning. After this job, there'll be bigger and better assignments. You'll be able to quit *The Inquisitor* and work on your books full-time."

He had it all figured out, their future all planned. Except he had neglected one important part. This trip wasn't a solid beginning; it was a convenient ending. He would never come back. Casey felt weak at the thought that this would be the last time she would ever kiss him, would ever see his face.

Whether Matt realized it or not, they could never have a lasting relationship. In a few weeks, maybe a month, he would realize it, too. The price of commitment was too high when the cost was his freedom. And she could never be happy with a vagabond like him and she loved him enough not to ask him to stay.

How many times had she begged her mother to stay? And each time, her mother would leave, needing to escape the bonds of responsibility, the prison of a home and family. Love was fine for a while, as long as it didn't require full-time attention. As long as there were no demands, no strings.

A man's got to be what a man's got to be, and Matt Garrison was a drifter through and through. Just like her mother. Casey had lived through the pain of her mother's desertion. She knew she couldn't live through another.

"Call me when you get back," she said, her voice trembling. "We can talk about it then."

"You'll be here when I get back? Promise?"

Casey nodded her head.

Then Matt pulled something from his pocket, placed it in her palm and wrapped her fingers around it. Casey opened up her hand to find a roll of film.

"It's the film of the wedding. You took the wrong roll." She reached out to touch the film still hanging around his neck. "Mule deer," he explained. "I want you to keep it. If you change your mind, I want you to give it to Griswold." Then he placed a business card beside it. "This is the photo editor's number at *World Geographic*. If you need to get ahold of me, for any reason, call him. He'll know how to reach me. I'll try to call you, Casey, but I don't know what the phone systems are like in rural China. And I'll write."

Casey handed the card back to him, knowing that it would prove to be too tempting. It was better to make a clean break, to burn all the bridges behind her. "I'll wait until you get back."

"No," he insisted. "I want you to call me immediately if you find out ... you know ... if you find out you're pregnant. Promise me that."

Casey looked at him in astonishment. "Pregnant?"

"I'm wounded that you don't remember the last time we made love, but we didn't use anything, remember? I just want you to know that I'll be there for you, in a second, if you need me. Promise you'll call me."

Casey nodded again, too stunned to speak. Oh God, he was right. They had gotten carried away. Could she be pregnant?

He drew her into his arms and kissed her deeply, interrupting her frantic speculation. "For the first time in my life, I don't want to leave," he murmured, burying his face in the curve of her neck.

Then he was gone, striding away from her to the waiting cab. She watched him walk away and etched the sight in her memory. You won't be back, she said to herself, already preparing her heart and mind for the hurt that lay ahead.

He turned around as if he had heard her thoughts and took a long, hard look, a crooked grin teasing his lips. "I know what you're thinking, Carmichael. And you're wrong. I will be back. I'm like a bad penny. And you will marry me. You can count on it." Then he stepped into the cab and it roared away, tires squealing as it turned the corner and took Matt Garrison out of her life as quickly as he had come into it.

CASEY PUSHED OPEN the glass door to the reception area of *The Inquisitor*. The familiar hustle and bustle greeted her and the receptionist smiled cheerfully as she walked in.

"Art's been looking for you," the young woman called out as Casey passed.

Art would have to wait. Casey made her way down the hall to her office. She found her cubicle and sat down at her desk. The room was empty as it often was late in the day when most of the reporters were out looking for stories or tracking down leads or gathered in their favorite bar in Venice.

She reached into her pocket, removed the film and placed it in front of her. It had been only three hours since Matt had placed the film in her hand and walked out of her life. Two and a half hours ago she had nearly thrown it down a storm sewer in front of her building. And now, she was actually considering turning the film over to Art Griswold.

Matt had realized his dream. He was off on an exotic and prestigious photo expedition, one that held incredible promise for his future. She, on the other hand, was no closer to coming up with the five thousand dollars she needed for the down payment on her dream. And now she had a possible pregnancy to worry about.

What if Matt was right? How could she expect to raise a child on her salary, working the hours she did? There was no question that she would raise the child, if there was one. But when she wasn't writing for *The Inquisitor*, she was writing for herself, leaving little time for motherhood. And having a baby was expensive. She doubted that her meager health insurance plan would cover all the costs.

She shook her head. Lord, she didn't even know if she was pregnant and already she was worried about how she was going to pay the medical bills. Over and over again in the past two hours, she had tried to calculate when her next period would begin. But dates like that had never meant much when there was no reason to worry about them.

Casey picked up the film and turned it in her hand. The ranch and Ellen and David seemed like a dream from the distant past. She held twenty-five thousand dollars in her hand: her future, and possibly the future of her child. Suddenly the money didn't just mean her dream, it meant survival. She had never been faced with such a choice before—friendship or survival, loyalty or life.

Casey flipped on her computer and began to type, her precisely chosen words filling the screen. She described Ellen's dress and the justice of the peace. She related Ellen's prewedding jitters and her comical attempt at muffins. The candlelight ceremony and the sprawling ranch house all became part of the narrative. And when she had finished she typed three # symbols to signify the end of her story.

Casey sat back and looked at her computer screen. She stared at the blinking green cursor for what seemed like hours, then scrolled back through the story and highlighted the contents. Then, with a sigh, she pressed the delete key and the story vanished from the screen.

She grabbed the film, stuffed it into her purse, and walked out of the office and down the hall to the reception area. She was almost out the door when she heard Art's call of greeting.

"Carmichael?" He strode up to her and gave her a gruff hug. "You're back! Where the hell were you? I asked everyone around here if they knew where you were, but no one did. B. J. Hopkins said you'd been abducted by aliens."

Casey smiled at Art. "I'm sorry I didn't tell you where I went. I guess I forgot to fill in the details. I was just checking out a lead on a story."

"The Harrington story?"

She shook her head. "No. A different story. It didn't pan out, anyway."

"Well, that's what I told the guy when he called last Friday. I told him you were working on a story."

"What guy?" Casey asked.

"That editor guy from New York. Nelson Cromwell Publishing. A persistent cuss."

"What?"

"Yeah, he called again yesterday. Said something about a letter." Art pulled a folded fax from his jacket pocket. "He seemed a little anxious so I had him fax a copy here. Thought I could read it to you over the phone if you called in. He left a number for you to call him back."

Casey fingered the curling paper, refusing to look at the letter. An urgent letter. From a publisher. And a phone call from an editor. Casey's heart was pounding and her pulse racing.

"Aren't you going to read it?" Art asked.

"I don't think so," Casey answered in a trembling voice. "Not right now."

"I think you should read it, Carmichael."

Casey drew a shaky breath.

"Read it," Art ordered.

Casey unfolded the fax and began to read.


Dear Ms. Carmichael,

Thank you for your recent submission of your detective novel, *Murder At Midnight*. Our editorial board has reviewed your work and we find it very promising. We believe that it would fit perfectly into our new line of paperback mystery

novels and would like to discuss the possibility of
publishing your novel.

I will be calling you within the next few days to
discuss the details of our offer. If you are working
through an agent, please let me know at that time.

We look forward to a bright future for both you
and Theodora Thibidoux at Nelson Cromwell.

Sincerely,
Donald Sinclair
Senior Editor

Casey glanced up from the letter, then turned for the
door.

"Carmichael, where are you going?" Art shouted.
"You're not going to quit on me, are you? Come back
here. Let's discuss this."

"I'll talk to you later, Art. I have a story to finish."

CASEY STARED OUT the window of the cab, watching the
numbers on each house in the lovely Beverly Hills
neighborhood. The unassuming Spanish-style homes
stood back from the street, surrounded by lush gar-
dens and by the obligatory iron fence. The houses
weren't as large as others in Beverly Hills, but they were
well guarded by huge gates that provided the only ac-
cess to the outside world.

It hadn't been hard to get Ellen's address. It was
common knowledge at *The Inquisitor*, as were the ad-
dresses of every other movie star worth a drop of ink
in the tabloid press.

The cab stopped in front of a modest house and
Casey stepped out, asking the cabbie to return in thirty

minutes. Across the street she noticed a group of three reporters, leaning against a car eating hot dogs. They stared at her, watching her every move distrustfully.

Casey walked over to them and pulled her press credentials from her purse. "Hi, I'm Casey Carmichael from *The Inquisitor*. Seen much action?"

"Naw," one of the reporters replied. "She went in this morning at about ten and hasn't been out since. We heard a rumor she was getting married, but from the look on her face when she got here, I'd say the wedding's off."

Casey leaned back against the car and studied the house. Then she sighed. "I don't know why I always end up on these dead-end beats. Why can't I follow the Liz story? Now there's a story that would make my career."

The reporters turned to her. "The Liz story?" the trio asked in tandem.

"Yeah, the whole office is buzzing. The boss sent three reporters and a photographer out. They say the marriage is over and she's dating an Arab sheikh. The biggest story of the year and I get stuck here."

She had barely finished her sentence before the three were running toward their cars. "Hey," she called after them for good measure, "where are you guys going?"

When the street had cleared and the reporters had gone, Casey walked to the gate and pressed the button on the intercom system. Several seconds later a familiar but angry voice answered her summons.

"I told you guys to leave me alone."

"Ellen?"

Silence.

"Ellen, it's me, Casey. Can I come in?"

"Casey?" Her voice was suspicious.

"Casey Car—Garrison." More silence. "I've brought you some new muffin recipes."

She heard a giggle through the speaker, then a buzzing sound as the gate unlocked. Casey pushed it open, stepped inside, then shut it behind her.

Ellen appeared at the front door, opened it a crack and watched as Casey approached. Casey could see the wide smile on her face.

"It's okay," Casey called. "You can come out. They're gone."

Ellen stepped outside slowly to confirm Casey's remark then ran across the lawn and threw her arms around Casey. "I can't believe you're here. When did you get in? Why didn't you call? Where's Matt? How did you get my ad—"

Ellen stepped back, then frowned. Slowly Casey pulled her press credentials from her pocket and held them up. Ellen's face turned white. "Your address is common knowledge at *The Inquisitor.*"

Ellen looked at her in stunned disbelief, her eyes wide like a frightened animal. Then she spun around and ran toward the house.

"We killed the story," Casey called.

Ellen stopped at the door and turned, her eyes mirroring her pain. "I thought you were my friend. I trusted you," she said in a shaky voice.

"I am your friend." Casey took a step forward. "And you can trust me. The story won't run." She took another step closer.

"You're a reporter."

"No, not anymore." Casey held her press card up and threw it into the bushes. "As of two o'clock this afternoon, I'm an author." She moved up the sidewalk and stood at the bottom of the front steps. "I'm sorry I deceived you, Ellen. I came here today to tell you the truth, for what it's worth. I know you can't forgive me, but that doesn't matter. I saw how happy you and David were and I just couldn't destroy that. I'm sorry. Please accept my apology for intruding on your life."

Ellen's expression softened slightly as she regarded her silently. "You—you sold your book?"

Casey nodded.

"And Matt? Is he really your husband?"

Casey shook her head. "He's a free-lance photographer."

"He's your boyfriend?"

Casey shook her head again, trying to stem the flood of pain that rushed through her. "No, he's—he means nothing to me. He's just a business associate."

Ellen looked at her. "I don't believe you."

"It's true, Ellen. We did kill the story. I swear."

"I mean about Matt. You love him and he loves you. You may have been pretending some things, but you weren't pretending that."

Casey felt tears stinging the corners of her eyes. She shook her head then reached up to swipe at one trickling down her cheek. "It doesn't matter. He's gone. To China. It's over." Casey sat down on the steps with a sob and buried her face in her hands. She felt Ellen's arm around her shoulders, and she looked up through tear-filled eyes.

Ellen smiled and patted her shoulder. "I think you and I should go inside and try out one of those muffin recipes. What do you say?" She pulled Casey up and gave her a hug. "And then you can explain to me how you're going to stop loving Matt Garrison."

## 10

*I filed my report with the police then drove up U.S. 1 toward Big Sur. Maybe a week away from L.A. would do me good. I had a stack of case files three feet high on my desk, but work was the last thing I wanted to do. It seems that each case takes a little piece of my soul, no matter how hard I try to keep my distance. This case took a piece of my heart, too.*

*Police cars blocked the road ahead. I pulled over and approached an officer who stood near the edge of the cliff. The remains of a mangled car lay a hundred feet below, at the base of the cliff. "His wife reported him missing last night," the officer explained. "We found the car this morning. Problem is, he wasn't in it."*

*"Maybe I can help," I found myself saying. "My name is Theodora Thibidoux. I'm a private investigator."*

*A woman's got to be what a woman's got to be. Isn't that how the saying goes?*

CASEY SMILED at her computer screen and reached out to pat the top of the terminal with her hand, as if it were a well-behaved pet. She hesitated for a moment, then typed in six more letters and a space.

THE END.

The cursor blinked, awaiting her next words. "That's it," she said with a trace of sadness. Like Theodora's cases, every book took a little piece of her soul. Each manuscript was like a child, the plot and characters nurtured carefully, until one day, the manuscript was ready to stand on its own. Then came the difficult process of letting go, of turning something very personal out into the harsh, cruel world.

Was that what it was like to be a mother? she wondered to herself. Letting go of a child must be much more painful than letting go of a silly manuscript. What had driven her own mother to run away as she had? Was she bored, or frightened, or confused? What had caused her to sever the natural bond between mother and child so cleanly?

Casey reached down to place her palm across her flat belly and tried to imagine what it would feel like to have a child moving within her. Two weeks after Matt had left, she had known she wasn't pregnant. She had found out on the same day that her contract had arrived from Nelson Cromwell Publishing. The happiest day in her professional life had become the saddest day in her personal life.

Twenty-four hours a day, for fourteen days, the anticipation had stayed with her. By the fourth day, she had known that she wanted a child more than anything in the world. Everything had fallen so nicely into place—her writing career, the purchase of her grandparents' home. But this time, good luck did not come in threes. She had her grandparents' house, she had a career as an author. But there would be no child, no family, no Matt.

Casey gazed out the wide picture window of the cabin to the porch and an ancient willow rocker, set in motion by the blustery spring breeze. Tiny buds were visible on the tips of every branch and the white ice that had covered the lake when she'd arrived six weeks ago had begun to melt, its hard surface now dark and slushy. Birds sang in the morning outside her bedroom window, and with the coming of spring, she could feel her dark mood begin to lift, like the sun breaking through on a dismal and cloudy day.

Punching the print command on her computer, Casey stood up and made her way to the bedroom to get dressed. She pulled out a bulky knit sweater from her dresser and had it on before she realized it was the sweater Matt had bought her in Laramie. Lifting the front of the sweater, she buried her nose in it and inhaled, hoping that some of his scent would still be present. But there was nothing, no reminder of him, except the memory of his concern for keeping her warm that night. She smiled sadly to herself as she put on her jacket.

Though spring was in the air, the half-mile walk into town was chilling. Her advance had provided the down payment for the cabin, but there still wasn't enough money for a car. When the road was covered with packed snow, she had taken an old sled into town to carry the groceries home. But now that the weather had broken, she had exchanged the sled for a red wagon.

The walk into town cleared her mind of the fogginess caused by three days of nonstop writing. As she walked down Main Street, Casey waved to Henry Winslow, the town barber, through the plate-glass window of his shop. She had accompanied her grand-father to Henry's shop when he had gone there for a haircut on the first Saturday of every month.

Lyle Elliot shouted a greeting from the front steps of Elliot's Hardware and Maggie Kelsey, the town librarian, beeped her horn as she drove by on her way home for lunch. Several more friends, both new and old, greeted her on her walk down Main Street. By the time she reached her destination, Casey was smiling, her step light and her mood brightened.

The tinkle of a bell sounded as Casey pushed open the front door of the post office. Addie Spenser, the postmistress, looked up from behind the wide, wooden counter. She grinned broadly when she saw the package that Casey carried.

"Well, what do we have here?" she asked as Casey slid the brown paper-wrapped box onto the counter. "Don't tell me this is another one of your books!"

"It's called *Murder on Monday*," Casey said with a nod. "I just finished it."

"Missy, you work too hard. This is the second book I've mailed since you got here."

"I wrote *Murder at the Mall* a year ago. My publisher asked to see it, so I polished it up. They may want to publish it after *Murder at Midnight* comes out."

Addie reached under the counter and placed a large manila envelope in front of Casey. "I been waitin' for you to come in. This arrived day before yesterday. Looks like it's important."

Casey ripped open the envelope and scanned the documents inside, then leaned over the counter with a shout of laughter and kissed Addie on the cheek. "It's

my contract for *Murder at the Mall*. It was the very first
Theodora book I wrote." Casey hugged the contract in
delight. "Another book means another advance.
Thanks, Addie. I'll see you tomorrow."

"You've been working awful hard, Casey, all cooped
up alone in that cabin, day and night," Addie called.
"Seems to me you need a break. There's a dance at the
Fireman's Hall two weeks from Saturday. Why don't
you come on down?"

Casey waved at her as she walked through the door
and continued to read the contract as she made her way
along the sidewalk to the grocery store, dragging her
wagon behind her. This time her arrival was signaled
by the creak of the front door as she entered.

Inside, the store was warm and peaceful and dimly
lit by sunlight filtering through dusty windows high
above the old plank floor. Casey closed her eyes and
drew a deep breath, letting the yeasty smell of fresh
baked goods mixed with the pungent aroma of pro-
duce play with her memory. She had accompanied her
grandmother to Spenser's Mercantile nearly every
Saturday of her childhood to help with the grocery
shopping.

"Mornin', Casey." Arlo Spenser, Addie's husband,
walked to the front of the store, wiping his hands on his
white apron and straightening the paper butcher's hat
that was perched on his balding head. "Addie told me
the good news. Says you sold another book. Folks here
in town sure are proud of you. Everybody's been askin'
if I'm gonna stock your book for them to buy."

Casey laughed, patting Arlo on the shoulder. "I think
that can be arranged, Arlo."

Addie Spenser had become her most ardent fan and a dedicated publicist. Without ever reading one of her books, Addie had turned Casey into a minor celebrity around town. Even the newspaper had run an article on her, then invited her to write a weekly book-review column. Casey took the job and learned later that it paid five dollars for each column she turned in.

It wasn't much, but it was a step up from *The Inquisitor*. She glanced over at the rack at the end of the checkout. Iowa Grandmother Gives Birth To Her Own Great-Grandson, the headline screamed.

Los Angeles was a distant memory now. In the past weeks, the pain of Matt's leaving had dulled to a tiny ache in her heart. They were never meant to be, she told herself over and over again, hoping to heal the hurt. It was better to make a clean break. Art was the only person who knew where she was, and he was sworn to secrecy. Art was an honorable man. As long as she wrote to him every week, he promised to keep her secret. It was a fair trade. Matt would never find her.

Maybe Addie was right, Casey thought to herself. Maybe she should get out more and meet a few people her own age, if there were any in town. As Casey left the grocery store, her eyes were caught by a poster for the Firemen's Annual Dance. She carefully noted the time. Dickie Jones and the Swing Kings were going to be playing. It looked like an event that shouldn't be missed.

THE SATURDAY OF THE Firemen's Dance turned out to be a glorious spring day with the temperature hovering in the mid-sixties. Casey had begun a self-imposed va-

cation several days earlier, after she'd finished final re-
visions on *Murder at Midnight*.

Over the past week, Casey had decided that Addie
was right. It was time to get out and socialize. Matt was
a part of her past now and it was time to look to the future. If she wanted a husband and a family someday,
she would have to put herself in the vicinity of the opposite sex.

She spent nearly an hour getting ready for the dance.
Her flowing cotton dress had come from one of the
boutiques catering to the summer resort crowd. The
pink-and-green flowered dress was very feminine, with
a wide sweeping skirt and a tight bodice. She tied her
curls back loosely with a pink satin ribbon, then slipped
into a pair of low-heeled pumps.

Casey walked out onto the porch and sat down in the
willow rocker to wait for Arlo and Addie to pick her up.
The balmy spring breeze rustled the currant bushes at
the base of the porch and the sun was just starting to set
over the lake.

The air around her hummed with the sound of insects and birds. In the distance, the lake lapped against
the shore, its calming refrain in counterpoint to the
chaotic songs of springtime. There was magic in the air
and for some reason, Casey felt a bit like Cinderella
awaiting her fairy-tale coach.

She closed her eyes and let the last golden rays of the
sun shine on her face. An image of dark windblown
hair and Pacific blue eyes rose in her mind and she let
the picture linger a moment, before she tried to bury it
in her subconscious.

The honk of a car horn from the driveway signaled the arrival of her ride and she jumped up, happy that her melancholy thoughts had been interrupted. She waved at Addie and Arlo as she approached the car, then got inside. The drive to the dance took just five minutes, not long enough to banish the disturbing image in her mind.

The interior of Fireman's Hall had been transformed into a wonderland of twinkling lights and crepe paper. A mirror ball twirled from the center of the ceiling, splashing droplets of gold around the dimly lit hall. Strings of tiny white Christmas tree lights were draped from the rafters creating the illusion of a starlit sky. The Swing Kings played "Moon River" as townspeople chattered and couples danced.

Casey was in the hall no more than a moment when she was approached by a hopeful dance partner. The word had spread, no doubt helped along by Addie and Arlo Spenser, that there was a single woman available and the area bachelors had turned out in force.

Elroy Schmitz was the first to claim a dance and spent his time informing Casey that he was the county's most successful farmer. By the time "Moonlight Serenade" was over, she knew the horsepower of his newest tractor and the name of his favorite milk cow.

"Stardust" was passed with Darwin Peabody who felt obliged to relay his mother's opinion of the state of popular fiction and the suitability of an author as a wife.

Scooter Davis, the town's resident jock and used car dealer, dragged her through an exhausting version of "On the Sunny Side of the Street," all the while bemoaning the fact that his ex-wife was bleeding him dry and his children didn't appreciate him. He concluded with an indecent invitation to accompany him home that evening.

Casey escaped the next bachelor in line by retreating to the shadows with a cup of punch and pretending to study a photo of the town's first mayor. She heard footsteps behind her and stiffened, fully preparing herself to refuse the next dance partner.

"Miss Lurleen?"

Casey spun around to find a timid-looking man standing before her.

"What did you call me?" she breathed.

"Aren't you Lurleen? My name is Edward Farley. I was wondering if I might have this next dance."

"My name isn't Lurleen," she explained in a choked voice as she stared at the man.

"It isn't? Why, that man over there told me your—"

"What man? Who told me my name was Lurleen?"

Edward turned and pointed across the hall.

Casey followed his direction to a tall form standing in the open door. It was the same image she had seen night after night in her dreams. She squeezed her eyes shut, willing the vision to disappear. This was just another dream. The only problem was, this time she wasn't asleep.

Casey slowly opened her eyes and he stood before her, his body outlined by the dim light of the hall, his features hidden by shadows.

"Lurleen," he said, his voice exactly as she remembered it, soft, teasing, seductive. "I thought it was you."

"Garrison," she murmured, "I thought I had gotten rid of you for good."

"You should know me better than that, Carmichael. You should have known I'd find you. I'm not about to let you back out on our deal."

"Deal?"

"You remember. A partnership. No more lies, no more deception, no more tricks. Equal partners, as I remember it."

She stood up slowly. "We tried that once before and it didn't work. What makes you think it will work now?"

He grinned, a heart-stopping, sexy smile that crumbled her waning defenses. "Trust me."

She laughed. "Trust you? Now where have I heard that before?"

"This time you can believe it." He reached out to touch her cheek, the warmth of his fingers melting the last traces of ice from her heart. "God, I love you, Casey. I've waited sixty-seven days, five hours and thirty-some minutes to tell you that. And I'm going to marry you."

"What if I refuse?" she asked.

"I'm fully prepared to hang around until you say yes."

"I guess I have no choice then."

"I guess you don't." Matt stepped forward and swept her into his arms, lifting her off her feet and twirling her around until she laughed in sheer joy. "You'll never get rid of me now, Carmichael!" he shouted, his voice rising over the sound of the band.

He buried his face in her neck and hugged her tightly, then his lips found hers and Casey was lost in his arms, drinking deeply of the taste and scent of him. It was as if they had never been apart, as if all the days of pain and longing had dissolved in a single moment and all the distrust and deception had never existed.

He had come back. He had kept his promise. And the waiting had made her stronger and more sure of her feelings. She was no longer an insecure child in need of a mother. She was a woman in love with a man. She held on to him more tightly, afraid to let him go for fear that he would disappear and she'd find this really was all just a dream.

Matt finally lowered her to her feet, then stood back and looked into her eyes. He captured her mouth again, kissing her long and hard and hungrily.

Casey pulled away and looked up at him. "I suppose I have Art to thank for your being here."

Matt shook his head. "Nope, he wouldn't talk."

"Then how—"

"He should know enough to lock his garbage up." Matt pulled an envelope out of his pocket. Casey recognized it as the one from her last letter to her old boss. "One never knows when an unscrupulous co-worker might go looking for classified information."

"You went through his garbage."

Matt nodded and smiled sheepishly. "I'm trying to change my ways, Casey. But I was desperate. I had to find you."

Casey stood on tiptoe and wrapped her arms around Matt's neck. "I don't want you to change, Matt, and I don't need you to change. I fell in love with a man with

a vagabond heart, and he's the man I intend to marry."
Casey touched her lips to his.

"So, this is it," Matt said, looking around the room.
"This is your dream."

Casey knew he meant the town, the people, her
home. Casey nodded. He was right, this was all part of
it, but there was more. She looked at him. "Yes, this is
my dream. Right here, right now."

The band began their version of "Isn't It Romantic"
and Matt grabbed Casey's hand and drew her out to the
dance floor. The crowd parted and stared at the couple, wondering who the stranger was and why Casey
Carmichael had thrown herself at him. A buzz of speculation swept through the room, but Casey was unaware of the talk she and Matt were creating. She was
captivated by the man who held her in his arms and
whispered words of love in her ear.

There was a time when she believed that twenty-five
thousand dollars could buy her dreams and she was
willing to do anything to get the money. But **now** she
knew dreams were priceless. They couldn't be bought;
they came to those who were patient enough to wait for
them.

# Epilogue

THE TINY PLANE STOOD at the end of the runway at the Northern Wisconsin Airport, propellers whirling and engines whining. Spring had finally arrived after a long, snow-filled winter and the fresh green scent of newly budded leaves was in the air.

Casey Garrison looked at her husband through shining eyes, then kissed him once again before she pushed him toward the open door of the plane.

"The sooner you go, the sooner you'll be back," she shouted.

"But what if I don't want to leave?" her husband complained.

"Matt, we go through this every time you have to leave on assignment. I'll be fine." Casey rubbed her protruding belly. "The baby will be fine. There's nothing to worry about. Ellen and David will be here for another week. If that's not enough, you have the town's entire population hovering over me whenever you leave."

Matt bent down and patted Casey's stomach through her bulky sweater. "You'd better stay in there until I get back, you hear me, little one?" He kissed her belly, then wrapped Casey in his arms again and took her breath away with his kiss.

"God, I can't stand leaving you. I love you."

"And I love you," Casey said, giving his hand a squeeze.

She watched as Matt ran to the door and hopped in, then waved as the plane began to taxi down the runway. She kept her eyes on the plane until it was a tiny speck in the southern sky.

There was no sadness in her heart as she stood on the deserted runway. The love that filled her soul left no place for loneliness. They were a family and he would be back.

All her dreams had finally come true.

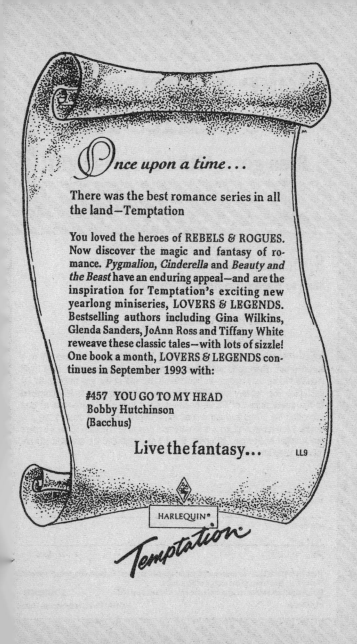

# Take 4 bestselling love stories FREE

## Plus get a FREE surprise gift!

# LIGHTS, CAMERA, ACTION!

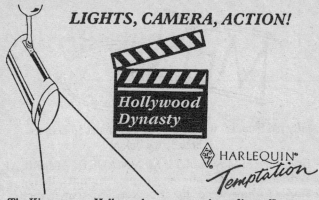

*Hollywood Dynasty*

HARLEQUIN®
*Temptation*

The Kingstons are Hollywood—two generations of box-office legends in front of and behind the cameras. In this fast-paced world egos compete for the spotlight and intimate secrets make tabloid headlines. Gage—the cinematographer, Pierce—the actor and Claire—the producer struggle for success in an unpredictable business where a single film can make or break you.

By the time the credits roll, will they discover that the ultimate challenge is far more personal? Share the behind-the-scenes dreams and dramas in this blockbuster miniseries by Candace Schuler!

**THE OTHER WOMAN, #451 (July 1993)**
**JUST ANOTHER PRETTY FACE, #459 (September 1993)**
**THE RIGHT DIRECTION, #467 (November 1993)**

Coming soon to your favorite retail outlet.

---

Fifty red-blooded, white-hot, true-blue hunks from every
State in the Union!

Beginning in May, look for MEN MADE IN AMERICA!
Written by some of our most popular authors, these
stories feature fifty of the strongest, sexiest men, each
from a different state in the union!

Two titles available every other month at your favorite
retail outlet.

In September, look for:

DECEPTIONS by Annette Broadrick (California)
STORMWALKER by Dallas Schulze (Colorado)

In November, look for:

STRAIGHT FROM THE HEART by Barbara Delinsky
(Connecticut)
AUTHOR'S CHOICE by Elizabeth August (Delaware)

**You won't be able to resist MEN MADE IN AMERICA!**

**Relive the romance...
Harlequin and Silhouette
are proud to present**

*by Request™*

A program of collections of three complete novels by the most requested authors with the most requested themes. Be sure to look for one volume each month with three complete novels by top name authors.

In June:  **NINE MONTHS** Penny Jordan
Stella Cameron
Janice Kaiser

**Three women pregnant and alone. But a lot can happen in nine months!**

In July:  **DADDY'S HOME** Kristin James
Naomi Horton
Mary Lynn Baxter

**Daddy's Home... and his presence is long overdue!**

In August: **FORGOTTEN PAST** Barbara Kaye
Pamela Browning
Nancy Martin

**Do you dare to create a future if you've forgotten the past?**

Available at your favorite retail outlet.

HARLEQUIN®  *Silhouette*

# Calloway Corners

In September, Harlequin is proud to bring readers four involving, romantic stories about the Calloway sisters, set in Calloway Corners, Louisiana. Written by four of Harlequin's most popular and award-winning authors, you'll be enchanted by these sisters and the men they love!

MARIAH by Sandra Canfield
JO by Tracy Hughes
TESS by Katherine Burton
EDEN by Penny Richards

As an added bonus, you can enter a sweepstakes contest to win a trip to Calloway Corners, and meet all four authors. Watch for details in all Calloway Corners books in September.

*(handwritten: (News Central \ US News CNN 17 Network)*

**Where do you find hot Texas nights, smooth Texas charm and dangerously sexy cowboys?**

*(handwritten: Favorite)*

*(handwritten: 70 / 170)*

### *HEARTS AGAINST THE WIND*

#### Strike it rich—Texas style!

Hank Travis could see himself in young Jeff Harris. The boy had oil in his blood, and wanderlust for the next big strike. There was nothing for him in Crystal Creek—except a certain marriage-minded Miss Beverly Townsend. And though Jeff seemed to have taken a shine to the former beauty queen, Hank wouldn't make book on Harris sticking around much longer!

CRYSTAL CREEK reverberates with the exciting rhythm of Texas. Each story features the rugged individuals who live and love in the Lone Star State. And each one ends with the same invitation ...

#### Y'ALL COME BACK...REAL SOON!
**Don't miss *HEARTS AGAINST THE WIND* by Kathy Clark**
Available in September wherever Harlequin books are sold.

---